Urban Folk Tales: Stories

by Y. Rodriguez

Published by

Read (v): The act of interpreting and understanding the written word.

Furiously (adv): To engage in an activity with passion and excitement.

Read Often. Read Well.
Read Furiously

Table of Contents

In memory of my parents, Silverio and Angelina Rodriguez,
and my sister Angelita Rodriguez-Finn.

Laura and the Kickboxer

David "El Caballo" Calderon waited impatiently for the N train in Astoria on 30th Avenue to head back into Manhattan. He had just met up with Joe, the bartender who worked at the jazz club on Steinway, about his gambling debt owed to his boss, Mickey "The Mouth" Maldonado, the big time numbers runner in the Bronx, Queens and parts of South Brooklyn.

David didn't like roughing up the customers, but it was the agreement between him and Mickey on how to deal with the losers who had no business borrowing money in the first place from guys like Mickey.

He didn't really hurt them anyway, just roughed them up a bit, a push and a shove, here and there, until they got the point. Thank God Joe had the money. Joe, a regular guy, who just fell on some hard times.

"I got the money right here, Dave. No hard feelings right?"

David took the money and placed it securely inside his vest pocket, almost ripped off from its seam from age and use. It reminded him to buy a needle and a spool of thread.

"No hard feelings, buddy. Stay out of the numbers racket."

He always warned them, all the gambling addicts, the ones who couldn't help themselves with betting on that million to one longshot to make it big. But in the end it was Mickey who would make it big when he'd send David out to collect on their debts.

David, an ex-kick boxing champion, felt that these jobs, even if they paid two hundred a day, were demeaning, lessening his championship memories of glory and pride, even if it's been nearly eight years since his last fight.

At least it paid the rent.

"Damn train. I'm gonna be fucking late again!"

David had already waited 20 minutes, losing his patience with each passing moment. Finally, the train pulled into the nearly deserted station hissing its own frustration upon the worn tracks.

It was the middle of the afternoon. David never kept regular hours, like the other working stiffs in the city. Nah, he liked it like this, working a little for Mickey, getting paid daily, and still having enough time left over for training. He was planning on making a comeback anyway, soon maybe, he just needed a little more time to make extra cash and get his two kids back. He didn't get a chance to prove to the judge that he was a fit parent, more fit than that stripper that he stupidly got pregnant and had to marry. Even after working a regular job as a security guard at a bank and then at night as a parking lot attendant, what did he have to show for it?

After the divorce he fought for custody but the judge ruled that a mother, even if she was an unstable alcoholic, was a mother nevertheless, and in the end more capable of taking care of the children than he. And then what happens, ha! The kids were taken from her after an ACS social worker made a surprise visit to find nothing but empty beer cans in the fridge and cigarette butts on unmade beds. The kids were sent to live with their maternal grandfather who cared for them.

Soon he would have enough cash in the bank from the jobs that he did for Mickey to prove that indeed he was the better parent after all and was more than capable of taking care of his own two kids.

The train finally arrived at the station and opened its languid doors.

"Miss, is this the N to Manhattan?"

The doors began to close as the young woman lifted her head from her book.

"Yes, yes, it is!"

But it was too late. The doors closed. But just in that very moment David noticed her attractive smile, so giving and welcoming. Just that one gesture, from a complete stranger, made him feel special.

David paused as the train remained motionless with its closed doors and he saw her again through the window, smiling at him. She shrugged her shoulders and shook her head at him, and then looked back down again to read her book.

Suddenly the doors magically opened. David lost no time to enter the car.

"Whoa! Made it!"

The train was empty and he could have sat anywhere in the car but he wanted to sit near her, the woman who miraculously opened the doors for him with her beauty.

"Mind if I sit here?"

She's afraid. He knew that he had blown it and moved away from her.

Cardinal rule #1 in subway riding: never make a woman

feel uncomfortable.

He noticed that she looked down the car to locate the conductor's booth. David noticed her relief.

He sat opposite her and waited before he spoke.

"Looks interesting."

The young woman held out the book. It was nearly half read.

"*The Autobiography of Malcolm X.* It's good."

She smiled again, but not like before, not a full teeth smile. This one was more like "leave me alone, I just want to read my book" polite kind of smile. David understood as he removed that morning's copy of the *New York Post* from his backpack.

"Let's see, ah, here it is, my 'horrible-scope.'"

The young woman looked up again. A kind look that embraced him.

"I'm a Cancer. And it sez here, 'Today you will meet someone who will help to guide your way.' Hmmm, that's interesting."

He peered his eyes over the paper, bespectacled, from the detached retina that he got ten years ago after losing a fight in Williamsburg.

"Does it really say that? Come on!"

It was an invitation, as he cautiously accepted it, rose and moved towards her, and sat close to her, but not too close.

"Yeah, look, right here."

He handed her the newspaper as she read. He noticed how pale her hands were.

"Yeah, you're right, thanks."

She returned the newspaper and went back to her book.

David was resolute.

"And what about you?"

"Me?"

"Yeah, don't you wanna know your 'horrible-scope' for today? Here, I'll read it. What's your sign?"

What a corny line! Couldn't he think of a better one?

"Pisces."

David's eyes widened behind his glasses making him look almost cartoonish.

"Pisces?"

"Yeah, anything wrong with that?" He liked her. Attitude!

"It just happens to be the most compatible sign to Cancer, that's all. Maybe this is destiny."

She rolled her eyes at him as the train continued in the tunnel, inching them closer and closer to their respective destinations.

"Okay, Pisces. For today, June 15, 1989: 'You have been having a run of bad luck but soon this will come to an end. Be patient and all your wishes will one day come true.' Wow, that's a good one. Look."

David handed her the newspaper as she read. Her short nails were kept manicured and polished, he noticed, not polished really, but buffed to a shine. He liked that. He admired women, and men, for that matter, who paid close attention to their personal hygiene. He was always around a lot of guys, fighters, who would never shower after a workout or a match and man, did they stink to high heaven! It was something that he was proud of; how he kept himself clean and well-groomed, even when he was at his poorest. Somehow this separated him from the others.

"Yeah, this is interesting. I hope they're right."

David took back the newspaper as he moved even closer.

Cardinal rule #2 in subway riding: never make a move if you think it's unwanted.

"Right? About what?"

She cleared her throat before she spoke; a smoker probably, he figured.

"Nothing, really. I'm on my way back from small claims court in Kew Gardens. The dry cleaners ruined my brand new leather jacket. I refused to pay the bill and then they didn't want to give me back my coat. So, I had to miss a day of work to fight it out in court with them in order to get it back. The judge asked us to meet again in a couple weeks since we couldn't agree to anything today, but luckily their lawyer convinced them to settle out of court or else waste another day and more money over such a minor thing. Anyway, so they agreed not to charge me and said that they would dry clean it again for free and fix the damage. An entire day wasted on something that could have been resolved weeks ago if they weren't so stubborn. What a waste!"

David didn't think this was a waste. He didn't think that the day was wasteful at all.

He knew what wasteful was, like that time after the divorce when he was cast in a small movie role as a stuntman. It paid real good, and it was a blast, the money, the women, but that's where his addiction started, with the coke and later the crack when he couldn't afford the real stuff anymore. Although he enjoyed all of it, for the most part, he really didn't as the casual sex and drugs made him feel soiled.

Now that was a big fucking waste of time.

But this, sitting here with her, it was heaven sent.

"Well, maybe you should look at it differently. We would have never met if you didn't take the day off to go to small claims court. Maybe we were meant to meet today for whatever reason, and I was meant to meet you like my 'horrible-scope' sez and one day maybe all your wishes will come true, if you're patient enough."

David wanted to say all of this but didn't. How could he? He just met her! She might think that he was one of those crazy subway people who mumble to themselves or flash passengers or ask for a handout. It would destroy everything--this moment, this special moment with her, right now, that maybe might lead to something else later. Nah, better to keep it all in for now.

Keep it light, keep it simple so that she won't leave him and sit somewheres else and he'll never see her again. "Then you won! You got your coat back! You're the champ! It wasn't a waste at all."

David knew that she looked at him now, really looked at him, noticing the color of his hair and its texture and how his glasses fitted around his face and how it made him look like John Lennon, (may he rest in peace), and the tan color of his skin and the shape of his mouth and how his teeth were perfectly straight and white and how he wore his jeans, tightly fitted around his sculpted legs and the shape of his forearms and the thick veins lining his large hands.

"Okay, maybe you're right. My name is Laura. Laura Miranda."

"I'm David. So, what do you do, Laura? I mean this job that you took the day off from?"

"Oh, my day job? I work in a hospital, in pediatrics. I'm

the assistant director in charge of the clerical staff. It's boring, but it pays the bills so that I can pursue my true calling."

"And what's that? Your calling?"

Laura looked down again at the book.

"I sing. I mean, I sing and I write music. Silly, uh?"

David moved closer to her, this time so close that he nearly shoved her off from the seat.

"Are you kidding? That's beautiful, man, I mean, Laura. That's really beautiful. What kind of music do you sing or write or whatever?"

Instantly he could feel her change, she was feeling him out, the distrust still there but diminishing.

"Original stuff, you know, stuff that I write, like pop, rock, blues and funk. I really love it but I especially like it when I see how the audience reacts to my music. Like when they start swaying back and forth to it, like it kind of puts them in…uh…like a trance or something like that. That's when I know that they like it, that they like me."

It was an urge that he felt; to kiss her, and kiss her hand gently, and hold it firmly in his calloused palm. He found it hard to resist doing it, right there and then. But he did. Resist.

"But it's a struggle, you know. Like sometimes we don't get the gigs and rarely do we ever get paid. So I have to work full-time, but I wouldn't trade it for anything else."

David knew exactly what she meant because that's how he felt about kickboxing.

He started out as a featherweight when he was only 15. As he moved up in weight and in rank and soon, after landing a lot of good punches and kicks, and having his brain mashed in a couple of times, he became the Middleweight Champion not only in Arecibo but also the statewide champ in New York.

But that was a long time ago and it's been a struggle ever since trying to get back to the light, trying to be a champ again.

"It's almost like breathing to me, my music. It's the only time that I truly feel alive."

David looked into her eyes and saw his, the way they looked back then.

It inspired him.

"I think I have to get off at the next stop for my transfer."

The sudden announcement of her departure made him curiously sad, as if he knew that if he didn't say something now, if he didn't act right now, he would never see her again.

"Listen, have you had lunch? I mean, we can get off just before we get into Manhattan. I know this little Greek diner on 31st Avenue where they make the best lamb shish kabobs, I mean if you like that, but they got a lot of stuff on the menu, if you want something else…"

David knew that Mickey would have to wait for his take from Joe and he knew that he would get pissed and maybe even dock him half his pay, but he didn't care. He didn't care at all now that he met Laura, and anyway, he was nearly ready to end his days with Mickey as the work was beneath him, an ex-champ, and an ex-champ shouldn't be hustling two-bit punks anyway for nickels and dimes, right?

Laura gazed at him. She knew that she had made a connection with the man as soon as he stepped onto the train.

She always has a thing for men who wear glasses.

"It's this place called Gus, and you could have anything. My treat, ok?"

The invitation both thrilled and flustered her. Laura had

been feeling a bit lonely these days since meeting Tony, the married guy that she started an affair with, just a few months earlier.

Their "on again, off again" romance, not including all of the wretched guilt that came along with it, brought her down.

David's interest made her feel attractive again and not as alone.

"Yeah, that sounds nice. I don't have to go back to work. I took the entire day off for this court thing. So, what do you do, David? David, right?"

What could he do but lie? What was he going to tell her, the truth? That he was a hired gun, not really, but something like that. Nah, better to lie, or tell her what he used to do.

"Look."

David opened his wallet and pulled out a worn out Screen Actors Guild card.

"I was in the movies, as a stunt man. I'm a trained fighter, so I do things like fighting stunts, punches and stuff like that and I can take a fall without hurtin' myself."

Laura held the card, impressed by its respectability. She took note that its membership expired five years earlier.

"It's real nice, David. So, you're a fighter. Wow! That's cool. Are you like Muhammad Ali?"

David laughed and adjusted his frames as Laura wondered how a fighter can win fights if he was near-sighted.

"Nah, nothing like him, although we do share something in common. We were both champs. I was a champion kickboxer in my prime. Look at this."

He removed a yellowing piece of newspaper tucked deep inside his black bi-fold leather wallet; the paper was chipped and crumbled like aging cheese in his hands.

"Look, this was here in the Bronx, in Fordham, after I won the fight against Jimmy 'The Beast' O'Connor. That's when I won the belt for kickboxing."

"Champion? Wow! You mean I'm sitting next to the champion? Wow! Like I've never met a champion before. That's so cool."

David took note of how young she was compared to his 40 years. Maybe in her late twenties at most, but she looked much younger.

"Nah, it's just me. I was almost 21 when I won and then that's when I started getting more fights and parts in movies and man, was I rollin' in the dough."

Laura had already noticed that one of the stems on his glasses had been bandaged, clumsily scotch taped to the frame like a tiny broken tree limb. She wondered why all of the prize monies had not gone towards the purchase of a new pair.

"After dat, well, you know, the fights stopped comin'. I was already over the hill, or so they said. But one day I'm gonna prove them wrong, Laura. You watch, one day I'm gonna be champ again."

And he meant it when he spoke of it to her, as if saying it out loud would make it real for him, would make it a vow that he would keep.

"I believe you, David. I believe you."

She savored the silence between them knowing that she too was ready to make a change, to forget about Tony at least for now.

"Come on, this is our stop."

Their lunch was both animated and short-lived as David's

incessant beeper kept interrupting them. "It's my boss, Mickey. I gotta go. But here." He scribbled something on a napkin.

"This is the only way to reach me. If you beep me, I'll get back to you"

"But how will you know that it's me who's calling?"

"Just put at the end of your number '615,' today's date, and I'll know that it's you."

"Thank you, David. I had a real good time."

David grinned as he counted out the tip, leaving more than double, feeling happy about the day with her.

"Listen, I spar with some guys at this little gym on East 79th and First. It's a church and downstairs they made this little sparring ring for some of us mugs, since one of our coaches is in their congregation. Why don't you come by tomorrow night at 8pm or so, and I can show you some of my moves."

"That sounds great, David. I mean, I don't have any plans, so I think I can make it." She lied.

She had promised to meet with Tony to discuss their situation but she was now determined to break it off, once and for all, and she promised herself that she would not allow her emotions to get the best of her.

"Great, Laura. I'll see you tomorrow."

It was more than great, it was thrilling, as David felt as if he was floating above the warm June pavement.

They moved ever so slowly, touching each other's elbows, on purpose and accidently, enjoying their time together, just him and Laura, during that day, as they made their way back to their separate homes.

David felt renewed. Ready to take on another fight. Ready to be champ again.

***

She never came.

After sparring with Joey "The Bull" Sanchez, one of the regulars at the gym and a retired kickboxer, David ran into the locker room to check his beeper. Not one call from her.

Not one "615" was registered on its tiny rectangular screen.

David wondered why he even bothered to give her his number, why he had even bothered to think that someone like her, so sweet and pretty and smart, would go for a bum like him.

All those punches to the cranium must have knocked his senses loose.

"Yo, man, that was a great fight."

Joey patted his back as he opened his battered locker.

"Yeah, I can see it, David, I can feel the comeback in those punches tonight. What happened to you? You on 'roids or something?"

David knew that a lot of fighters, the lazier ones especially, who didn't want to bother with the extra push-ups and chin-ups and sit-ups and sparring matches, and whatever it took to get stronger and faster and better, chose the drugs instead.

David knew better after kicking crack that such things were better off left alone as they would either make you fucking lose your mind or kill you. Neither was an option that he cared to consider.

"Nah, man, it ain't that. Just some girl that I met yesterday. I invited her, you know, to watch, but I guess she changed her mind."

Joey twisted and turned his body to wrap a white towel that read *St. Michael's Gym* around his expanding fleshy belly.

"Aw, don't let it bother you, man, maybe she got caught in traffic or had some kind of 'mergency, or some shit like that. You know how girls are."

David wondered what girls were, even after all these years. Or maybe he never really knew what a girl really was, until he met Laura.

"Yeah, that's true. You know I met her on the subway and she was coming back from small claims court. Yeah, I never thought of that. Maybe she had an emergency. Thanks, Joey."

Joey removed his towel and jumped into the torrent of warm water.

"Yeah, maybe she'll call you later, man. Gotta have that faith, man, if you're gonna be a champ again."

David began to remove his clothes cheered by his friend's words, uplifted once again, as he felt yesterday when he left her, as he allowed the shower's water to fill him with a restored hope.

***

Laura knew that she had hurt David as soon as she agreed to see Tony again that night.

And it pained her almost as if someone had inserted a sharp pin under her skin; a pinching hurt, raw and long lasting.

She agreed to meet Tony where they would usually meet at the café in Washington Heights, far enough away from his downtown neighbors and his wife. As she sat, in their usual booth, she noticed a pay phone, thinking of David as she fingered the loose change in her leather jacket.

Tony was late, as always.

Laura began to feel her life slipping away with each passing minute, wasting her time for a man in a diner who was unavailable. And she waited, probably like how David was now waiting for her, as she continued to fiddle with the three quarters that she always carried around just in case of an emergency. She rose and sighed as she headed for the pay phone to call David.

"No more waiting around for nobody!"

And in that same moment Tony entered the diner, looking flushed and bursting with readied apologies.

"I'm sorry, negrita, please forgive me."

He reached for her as he would always reach for her and kissed her deeply, leaving her feeling light-headed and confused.

"Tony, please."

She gently pushed him away still tasting his bitterness; a hint of black coffee and familiar excuses.

"What? So, what? I'm a little late. So, kill me!"

"You're not a little late, you're always late."

Laura reached for the quarters again, loosening her grip as she let them fall inside her pocket.

"Come on, let's get something to eat. I'm starving."

In the booth, he grabbed her arm and looped his arm into hers, a reversed bridal march grip.

"Come, on, hon, we're gonna need our energy for later."

He stuck his tongue into her ear. Laura pulled away feeling stained, knowing where the night would lead if she allowed it.

"Is that all there is for us, Tony? A quick fuck and back to the wife and kids?"

Tony pulled her away as he, on reflex, searched the menu.

"*Ssh,* you want the world to know our business. You know I love you, baby, you know that we talked about this before. I can't do anything until…"

"Until what, Tony? Until what? There is no 'until' because 'until' is something that you promised your wife, 'until death do us part,' remember?"

Laura searched for the coins again. David. "Listen, I gotta go, I promised this friend…"

Tony embraced her again, gently and firmly, in his strong arms, and kissed her.

"I thought I was your friend, Laura. Please let's not fight. You know how things are. You know that you gotta give me time to work things out so that nobody gets hurt, you understand? Please trust me."

He kissed her again and this time she returned it.

"That's it, my baby. Come on, let's get out of here and go back to your place. I've been waiting to get between those beautiful legs of yours all day and you know what I'm going to do, right?"

He nuzzled in her hair and kissed her neck with the tip of tongue, exciting her, as she surrendered to him once again.

"Come on, honey, you know I love you and I know you love me."

He was right about that. She did love him. But was it really love?

"Okay, Tony. Let's go."

They made their way out of the diner and walked back

to her studio apartment, downtown, where they would unfold the sofa bed and make love into the night, until it was time for him to leave, as he would always leave, leaving her alone, again, promising to one day make it alright between them.

Laura stood alone dressed in her bathrobe as she collected her clothes from the floor and noticed that the three quarters had fallen from her pocket. Lost coins. Lost chances.

She thought about David as she wept.

In that moment she promised herself that things would finally change.

***

Mickey "the Mouth" Maldonado sat in his torn fake leather office chair shifting himself back and forth in the seat, as he spoke.

"Where can a man get a good cup of coffee around here?"

Petey "The Pauper" Barrios, his long-time aide, a diminutive, sweet-natured man, shambled into the office at the request.

"What can I get you, boss?"

Mickey chomped on his unlit cigar as he searched the mess of newspapers that littered his desk.

"I need a light, my cigar's out. And where's that guy, David? Where the hell is he? I need him for another job. Beep him, call him, and tell his broke-ass, pathetic self to get over here now! Where are my fucking matches?"

"Here you go, boss."

"Thanks, Pete. Now where's my coffee? And don't forget

about dat bum. He's too much of a chicken shit to even get my money back for me. What's a man gotta do around here to make an honest livin'? Damn, I give youse guys all the breaks and all I ever get is a fucking headache. I'm too much of a push over."

Petey stared at his boss, noticing how large he had grown in the middle, looking like a Puerto Rican Pillsbury doughboy with a deep dark tan and graying hair and mustache that he would dye black from time to time. Petey wanted to laugh but he didn't.

"Go get me some coffee, Petey, and go call that bum. I got a lot shit to take care of today."

Mickey handed him some cash.

"And don't forget to get yourself something too, Pete."

Petey liked Mickey even if he treated him like crap, every now and then. Overall Mickey was a nice guy deep down, for a numbers runner that is.

"Sure thing, boss."

Petey opened the door just as David entered wearing the New York Yankees cap that Petey got him for Christmas last year.

"Well, well, well, lookie here, Petey. If it ain't 'El Caballo' himself!"

"Hey, Dave. When you gonna make a comeback, Champ?"

Mickey laughed at Petey's question, loudly, gagging, nearly choking himself with the stubby piece of tobacco.

"Come back? Come back? Are you fucking kiddin' me, Petey? This guy who can't even muscle a guy for a few bucks? You think he's gonna make a comeback? The day that hell freezes over is when this little nobody will make a comeback and that's never. Now get my coffee. I gotta talk to David." Petey nodded sadly to David as he turned to leave.

"Good luck anyway, Champ…"

David was appreciative of Petey's support even if Mickey was right. But Mickey wasn't right and David will one day prove him wrong.

He didn't want Laura to know what he did for a living and he was going to end it all with Mickey today.

Make a fresh start. With her.

"Wass'up up Mickey?"

Mickey looked at one of the newspapers as he chewed. Never once looking up to address David.

"Look at this, Dave. It says here that some dumb ass lucky guy in Brooklyn just hit the Powerball. $10 million dollars! Ain't that something?"

David shifted nervously in his seat as he began to feel his beeper vibrate in his pocket. Was it her? Finally?

"And you know what? He's gonna get every bit of that money that he won because the state runs the lottery, so it's all fine and legal, even if it's still gambling. But me, I'm the little guy, I'm the guy they wanna squash like a fucking roach, the one who makes his pennies helping our people in the slums find their American dreams with a lucky winning number. But some of those customers, you know they get a little carried away sometimes, and they spend too much money on a bet when they don't really have the money to spend, so they come to me and me, I'm such a softie, you know, I take pity on them, our people, and loan them the cash that they need to place the bet, but they're ingrates, Dave, they forget how I helped them in the pinch, so you know how much it hurts me to have to use a little muscle just to get back my money. You follow me?"

David reached into his pocket and looked at the tiny screen. 615. Laura!

"David, pay attention!"

David placed the beeper back inside his pocket. His body tingled excitedly, an internal fire set by the simple message.

She did care.

"Listen, I'm gonna give it to you straight, Dave. You're fired!"

David could barely hear Mickey's words as his heart nearly jumped right out of his chest from excitement. Maybe there is hope. Maybe he can make a comeback. Maybe he will be happy.

"Are you listening to me?"

"Listen Mickey, you're right to fire me! But I wanna thank you for helping me with everything, but this life, well, it ain't for me. I'm a fighter and I gotta fight. I ain't no punk, and I ain't no thug hustling poor slobs for you. This is all I got."

David held out his hands, still bruised from the sparring with Joey.

"This is what made me a champion once and it's gonna make me a champion again, Mickey. Listen, I gotta go. I got some training to do."

Mickey jumped from his seat as his cigar fired out of his mouth like a tiny submarine missile.

"Get out of my office, you ungrateful bum! All the shit I done for you! Keeping you off the streets away from those crack whore friends of yours and this is how you repay me? You lousy bum!"

"But you fired me!"

"Yeah, but you're not supposed to agree with me!"

David placed his hand in his pocket to touch the beeper, nearly seeing her face before his eyes.

"I gotta go, Mickey. No hard feelings. Thanks for everything man but I ain't no bum. I can't muscle guys for you no more, Mickey. Try one of those Codero brothers from the Bronx, you know the ones who do extreme fighting. It just ain't my style."

David remembered that there was a phone just down the block, on the corner, one of the few working public phones in that part of the Bronx.

"I gotta go, Mickey!"

David ran past Petey who was just returning with the coffee.

"Hey, champ, where you goin?"

"I gotta go, Petey. And don't let Mickey push you around."

Mickey retrieved his cigar and chomped down on it hard; David was right about those two nasty brothers in the Bronx; they'd fucking kill their own mother for a buck. He vowed to call them later.

"That poor slob Caballo, Petey, he got some loco fantasy about a comeback. What a fucking joke! He's fuckin' wastin' his time, right Pete?"

"Whatever you say, boss. But I think he's gonna be champ again one day. Who knows?"

Like a rat, Mickey sniffed at the small brown paper bag that held the cup of coffee.

"Petey! You forgot the fucking cream!"

***

They returned to the Queens diner where they shared their first meal.

"It's nice to see you again."

David dipped the French fry into a small pile of ketchup on his plate, not really hungry. Too happy to be hungry.

"I'm really sorry about the other night, David. Something came up."

He knew just by looking at her that there was more to her story, more than he cared to know at this point. He was just grateful that she was there now, right now, with him, eating good greasy food, and looking into her multi-colored eyes that changed from brown to gray in the sunlight.

"Ah, don't worry about it, it's no biggie. But I have to say that you missed a damn good sparring match between me and my boy, Joey."

Laura tried to conceal her guilt in her food about her date with Tony. It pained her to hurt him.

She didn't want to do it ever again. She called Tony and broke it off. "I have to find my happiness," she explained. And she never heard back from him again.

"Did you win?"

"Yeah, big time, Laura. It made me feel like maybe I'm finally ready for a professional match. Joey's also my part-time manager so he's gonna hook me up in one of the smaller arenas in Brooklyn first and then we'll make our way back to the Garden, you know, big time, like before."

David bit into one of the chicken fingers savoring the decision to return to pro fighting, and to one day maybe regain his championship belt after all those years.

"That's great, David. I know you'll win again. I just know that you'll become a champion again."

She grasped his hand and placed it into hers almost on instinct. And he embraced her gesture, kind and soft.

"You're a sweet girl, Laura. I don't think I ever met anybody like you."

He could see her blush as she drank her Diet Coke.

"Come on, we better hurry before the movie starts."

The comedy was a good pick by Laura who wanted to forget her sorrow about Tony and enjoy her time with David.

"I had a great day, David. You really make me feel happy. So, I guess this is good night."

Laura stepped forward to kiss his cheek as he turned and made a quick connection with her mouth. They kissed deeply. And he stayed in her arms throughout the night, as they stopped and started again with their embraces and held each other into the night, until the morning came to wake them.

David spent the next weeks seeing Laura and training with Joey feeling stronger and stronger with each passing day and each fight. She was his inspiration and the source of a recovered strength that he would need for his comeback fight.

"El Caballo is back!"

Joey was good at reminding him of this as the days of training came and went, uncovering the fighter that was buried beneath the years of neglect and David felt it, like electricity from a power plant filling him up, step by step, day by day, kiss by kiss, whenever Laura would accompany him to the gym, until he finally thought about something that he had not even dared to think about in the last few years– that perhaps he might be champion again.

"Listen, Caballo, I got you that fight with that kid Gonzalez, in Brooklyn next week but you gotta promise me to protect yourself, okay? He got two things over on you, Dave, youth and speed."

David removed his gloves as he prepared for a hot shower. He knew that Joey was right and that he had to protect himself.

He'd seen other fighters his age, wanting to make a comeback, their teeth bashed up inside their skulls by the first round. He had to now fight with his smarts, rather than rely on the mechanics and brawn of fighting which he knew were harder to trust as he aged.

"But I gotta tell you, buddy, you got a few things over that kid. Power, resiliency and heart! I ain't seen nobody in my life like you, Dave; you can take a fucking punch and still get right back up for more. That's what makes great fighters, Dave, that's what makes champions and I believe in you, man."

The water felt good on his sore body as David thought about his dinner date with Laura that night, and how he would fight for her and win for her, because she deserved that and he deserved that.

To win the fight. To get his kids back. To fall in love. To be happy.

He was supposed to meet her at 9pm but he still had not received her call on his beeper.

David thought back to that day when she missed his sparring match with Joey and hoped that she hadn't changed her mind about everything, about him.

"Have a good night, buddy and I'll see you here again tomorrow night. Say hello to Laura."

David knew that Joey was a good guy; he was lucky to have him in his corner. David looked at his beeper again.

Still no call.

"And don't forget, that around this time next week my friend, you will be a contender for the middleweight championship belt in kickboxing again and ain't nobody gonna say any different. Good night."

David waved his goodbye. He decided that he would call her at home as he somberly made his way down the corridor.

"David!"

She came in out of breath, soaked with that evening's rain.

"The N train got stuck at 59th and Lexington Avenue so I decided to walk. I'm sorry I'm late - "

But before she could finish he swept her in his arms and kissed her.

"No, baby, you're just in time."

WAITING FOR DR. WU

Long ago, he promised himself that he would never fall in love with any of his patients.

It was forbidden, it was wrong; a true violation of the patient's trust, and a complete betrayal of his own beliefs.

He was a doctor, after all, a noted physician and respected surgeon in his field.

He saves lives, for God's sake! First do no harm, right?

But then she walked in.

Long, flowing black curls, like tiny ringlets of Mediterranean black olives linked together, swept down and overflowing like a waterfall around her lightly tanned oval face; a short young woman, but slim and curvy, Venus-like.

As he entered the examining room, where she sat in those God awful gowns, she looked like an uncomfortable Latina Princess perched up on a stone; a touch of impatience filling out her lower pouty, lip.

He could not help but be charmed; how she greeted him with a sincere face, as he walked towards her, hand extended, shiny white teeth, straight and aligned, with her face lifted up, so slightly, resplendent in the otherwise unflattering fluorescent examination room light.

No make-up, not a trace.

Her long, straight eyelashes fluttered nervously, resembling two wounded butterflies, as she spoke.

He felt an instant attraction, but suppressed it, extinguishing the danger of feeling such a thing.

It shamed him.

"Miss Martinez?"

She was barefoot as she sat ready to step into the barbaric cold, steel stirrups on either side of the examining table.

He often wondered why someone could not invent a more humane way to conduct a pelvic exam.

Haven't women already suffered enough?

Apparently not.

He gently touched her knee.

She shot a glance at his attending nurse.

"Don't worry, Miss Martinez. I don't bite."

She was cute, but he dared not to give it another thought.

Too risky.

"What can I do for you, Miss Martinez?"

The girl shifted her bottom on the paper lined table using it to steady her anxiety, crossing her arms defensively against her breasts.

Despite how hard she tried to hide it, he could tell how lovely she was.

He quietly scolded himself for thinking such things.

"Dr. James, he sent me here. Your colleague."

"Yes. He's a good doctor."

"Well, he told me…"

"Yes, he told me, too…"

She looked at his nurse again; too many people in the tiny space, she thought.

After all, her cancer diagnosis was something that was her diagnosis.

Why should she have to share it with anybody other than Dr. James and now Dr. Wu?

Is that his name? Is that his name - Wu?

She looked into his eyes that peered past and over his oversized 1980s Elton John frames.

Kind eyes.

His stature, short and a bit overweight.

A cute, little Buddha.

Would he bless her?

Would he save her life?

"Dr. James, he performed a biopsy, and he saw it, from the sample that he took…cancer. Stage One. Uterine."

She looked over the nurse who turned slightly away, suddenly making the world a very sad place.

She wanted to cry, but not in front of him.

Dr. Wu stared into her eyes. Steady and confident. Listening.

She liked him.

He wasn't afraid.

"I saw the biopsy, Miss Martinez. Nothing to worry about, ok? First things first.

"Ok."

The exam hurt as she still had not yet healed from Dr. James' exam.

He felt her flinch as he continued.

"I'm sorry, Miss Martinez. Almost done."

The instrument was cold as it entered her, pinching her inside, making her want to scream.

But she was strong.

She could take it.

"Okay, we're all done. Now my nurse is gonna take some

blood. It's for an indicator that we use to test the level of white blood cells. You're gonna be okay, I promise."

Is she in shock?

Probably from the diagnosis.

Post-trauma.

He's seen it before.

"Ok, Miss Martinez?"

She became brave for him. Wanting to cheer him up. She never wanted anyone to suffer or to be unhappy on her account.

Their happiness always comes first. Like she was taught.

Never to be selfish or self-absorbed.

Even when she was at her most vulnerable and fearful, she needed to reassure everyone else around her that everything was going to be okay.

Maybe it was time that she did this for herself?

"You're a good girl. I can see that."

He called her a girl! She was nearly 40.

"You're young. You have your whole life ahead of you, Miss Martinez. You'll be okay, ok?"

She tried smiling again, wanting to feel as confident as the good doctor.

"Okay."

"Now you can get dressed, and then go to the lab so that they can take the blood. Let's make another appointment for next week, ok?"

He offered his hand as she enveloped hers into his, feeling a great warmth.

Reassured. Positive. Safe.

He noticed her eyes again.

The light therein. Very bright.

She was a passionate woman.

He could tell.

A grounded, beautiful woman.

"Okay."

She slipped her hand away from his as she climbed down.

"See you next week."

He turned from her.

Her simmering heat lingered in his palm.

It was dangerous.

He could not do this.

He couldn't have feelings for her, nor for any of his patients.

They are his patients. Under his care.

He promised that he would fortify himself that evening with a stiff scotch and maybe some vodka. Maybe pick up that girl, the hostess at his favorite restaurant.

It would make him remember who he is.

She dressed as they left her alone in the office.

Now she'd have to wait another week. Another long week of waiting.

More bad news.

She was sure of it.

***

Dr. Wu rushed her results.

His friend, Dr. James, was an exceptional doctor. Even without a microscope he would always be right about these things.

The tests showed a malignancy and an unusually high white blood cell count.

James was right.

Damn it!

He knew that he couldn't waste any time and scheduled the surgery for the following week. He had to determine the stage of the cancer as soon as humanly possible and then go from there.

He'd probably have to remove everything.

Damn!

Too young.

He remembered Amy.

Just 21 years old. Recently married.

She was 8 weeks pregnant.

They had to abort the baby to try to save her life.

Stage Four ovarian cancer.

Worse kind.

Almost no chance of survival.

He picked up Miss Martinez's chart.

"Emily," he whispered her name.

Pretty name.

Hopefully it didn't move outside the uterus.

Hopefully the surgery would be enough.

She was pretty.

That hair.

So black, that it was almost blue.

So thick, and long, and charmingly curly.

He might have to tell her that she might lose it all.

Because of the chemo.

But maybe not.

He'd know once he took a look inside.

He stopped crying long ago.

But still it got to him.

The drinking helped a little.

It kept the insomnia and nightmares at bay.

But it was never enough.

It was his choice.

He had an affinity for surgery, a born natural surgeon, as his mentors and teachers would tell him.

But ultimately he knew that it was always in God's hands.

He always had to remind himself that.

Sometimes they were things that were beyond his skills.

Dr. Wu picked up the phone.

"Nurse, you can send her in."

She had been waiting since early that morning.

Too many patients, not enough time.

He saw Amy and her fiancé earlier.

The new chemo drug wasn't working.

It was making her too thin, too weak.

But she remained cheerful, despite being eyebrow-less, eyelash-less, and completely bald.

She was sweet.

Engaged to a large, tall, guy named Mike.

Big Mike.

They invited him to their wedding that coming weekend in the Hamptons at her parents' home.

He loved the Hamptons.

That's where he met his ex-wife.

A pretty blonde.

They had three children.

All mixed-raced.

Beautiful.

But the life of a surgeon proved too hard for her.

He had no personal life. No time for a family.

His entire life was at the hospital.

Saving lives. Losing them.

Fighting the scourge.

Winning sometimes.

Losing sometimes.

Such is the life of a cancer surgeon.

"Ms. Martinez! Hello! How are you?"

She came armed.

A boyfriend? Or maybe her husband?

No, she listed herself as single on the pre-admit form in her chart.

A boyfriend.

Sure, of course she'd have one.

She was gorgeous.

But the type that would never know how beautiful she really was.

"This is Luis, Dr. Wu. I hope you don't mind…"

"No, no, not at all, please sit. Welcome!"

Luis' grasp was firm.

He meant business.

Dr. Wu sat back down on his chair feeling twitches of jealousy, disappointment.

That's stupid!

He was now her doctor.

He was now in charge of saving her life.

Nothing more.

He was glad that she had a boyfriend.

More distracting.

Now he could really concentrate on her treatment.

"Hello, Luis. Nice meeting you."

A tough guy, maybe too tough for sweet Emily. "Likewise, Dr. Chu. So, what's up with Emily?"

"Dr. Wu."

"Yeah, right. So, what's up with Emily?"

He was happy for her.

Happy that she would have a shoulder to cry on.

"Let me cut to the chase. Dr. James was right, Emily. It is cancer. I'm sorry."

She did not bow her head, or turn away from him, like some of his other patients. Some cried just at the mention of the word.

She was brave.

"What do we do?" the boyfriend asked.

Dr. Wu liked him.

No BS about him.

"Surgery. We'll have to remove the uterus, Emily." She was 39. Still no kids. He felt sorry for her. She seemed like someone who'd make a nice mommy.

"Okay. Anything else," she spoke softly.

A sweet dove.

"Well, hard to say right now, until I can take a look inside. But hopefully, Dr. James is correct that it is only stage one. If that's the case, there's no need for additional treatments. The surgery would be enough." He looked at her hair.

That hair.

It would be such a shame to lose it all.

But like he always told all of his patients: it will grow back!

"I scheduled you for surgery for next week…8a.m., here at the hospital. Bring your family….or your friends. Or Luis here.

The more the merrier. Don't worry about anything.

Just relax. Nothing to worry about yet, ok, Emily?" There he goes again! Blah, blah, blah, blah, blah and more blah.

Was this his way of staying sane or his way of keeping them sane?

"Okay, Dr. Chu. Next week."

"Dr. Wu."

"Yeah, ok. Next week."

They rose to leave as she turned to shake his hand.

"Thanks again, Dr. Wu." He felt it again.

His flesh shivered.

It scared him, in a terribly strange and thrilling way.

Had he finally met "the one?"

"Next week, Emily. Luis, take care of her, ok?"

"Yeah, Dr. Nu...uh…Chu…"

"Dr. Wu…like Sue, Luis. Wu."

"Oh yeah, sorry…"

He was an idiot!

How could she be with someone like that?

He dismissed the thought. How could he make that judgment?

He was her doctor.

He laughed at Luis' ignorance.

"It's Chinese." Luis laughed.

What a dummy!

What did she see in him?

Careless thoughts.

He'd have to keep himself in check.

He was there to save her life.

Not show his true feelings.

Towards her, or for anyone.

It was the only way to keep his hands from shaking.

***

Amy's wedding was beautiful. It was mid-June.

Perfect day.

Sunshine.

Not too warm.

She wore white.

The groom cried.

Dr. Wu made a toast to the happy couple. "May you live a long and happy life together." He lied.

She had only a few weeks, perhaps not even that.

He told her finance about it, in his office earlier that week.

"There's nothing I can do at this point, Mike. It's in God's hands."

But too much chemo and radiation had already taken a toll on the petite woman's body.

It was time to stop.

Keep her from suffering any longer.

But he knew, deep down, that she knew that it was near the end.

That's why she wanted to get married.

"It's something that I always wanted, Dr. Wu," she once whispered through the unbearable pain of another chemo session.

"A beautiful white wedding, with all of my friends and family. It'll be good for Mike, too. It'll help him, you know?" She knew it was over.

Dr. Wu found a seat under a shaded oak.

He looked through his appointments for the following
Monday.

"Surgery. Emily Martinez. 8am."

He sighed as he thought about her.

Another lovely girl.

He hoped that she would fare better.

That's what he hoped for all of his patients.

One would outlast the next.

But these days he saw more and more of them in his office.

Almost an epidemic.

Was it the water?

"Dr.?"

He looked up at the waiter.

Nice wedding.

A catered affair; courtesy of Amy's wealthy parents.

Their only child.

Not even their money could help her now.

"More champagne?"

Dr. Wu happily took the drink.

"Thanks!"

Cheers!"

He would drink for the rest of the weekend.

Might as well have a little fun, some joy, for now at least.

The band, a full orchestra, began a lively waltz.

The bride and groom danced the first dance.

Perhaps their last.

From where he sat, he toasted them again.

"Here's to the happy couple!"

Then he thought about her again.

"Emily Martinez."

He never did this before.

Obsessed.

Well, not really *obsessive*.

But her beauty lingered, her image relaying itself in his mind's eye.

Why?

He drank again.

"Waiter! Another please!"

He had to struggle against his feelings for her.

What was it about her?

He just couldn't stop thinking about her.

"Thanks."

He emptied the goblet.

Cold, crisp French Dom Pérignon.

He used it to clear his mind of her.

But it didn't work.

It only helped him to think more of her.

Maybe some coffee.

He looked at his watch.

It was still early.

The kids were with their mom this weekend.

What would he do tonight?

He looked through the directory in his smartphone.

"Tanya…nah, too high maintenance."

He looked at other names but returned to his Monday appointment with Emily.

"I have to stop this."

He stood and walked towards the newly married couple.

"May I cut in?"

He took the dying bride into his arms.

"You look lovely, Amy. Your dream came true today."
"Thanks to you, Dr. Wu. Thanks for keeping me alive this long."

The song was about lasting love, and eternity.

He knew, holding her, that Amy's spirit would always be everlasting. "You're welcome. Anyway, it wasn't all me, Amy. You're a real fighter…"

Indeed she was.

Two years of aggressive chemo, and one of radiation. Most people wouldn't be able to get out of bed, let alone attend their own wedding. She kissed him on the cheek.

"Thanks, Dr. Wu. You're awesome!"

That's what the others would always tell him before they left this world.

Where was the anger and the bitterness?

"Don't worry, Dr. Wu. You did your best," she whispered. "Like you told Mike it's in God's hands now. Let's have fun today, ok?"

"Ok, Amy. God bless you."

They danced until he handed her over to Mike.

He wanted to cry. But he didn't. He couldn't.

He knew that he could never cry.

It would not be appropriate.

Not now.

Not ever.

It was indeed a lovely wedding.

Within a few days, Amy passed away in her sleep.

*****

Emily arrived early with Luis.

Her siblings would come later.

"You're all registered, Miss Martinez. You can change in the locker room and leave your possessions there." She never had surgery before. Not like this. She had her tonsils removed when she was nine but that was about it.

"I'll be in the waiting room when you get out, ok?" Luis' cell phone rang again. It always rang.

"Hello? Yeah, hey, 'bro…listen hold on! I'm at the hospital with Emi."

He kissed her cheek and almost gave her a little shove.

"Don't worry. Everything will be alright."

He turned his attention away from her.

"Yeah, we gotta get those guys back on the picket line…"

He worked for a union. An organizer. Someone who served the greater good, but had difficulty taking care of her. But one thing that she always appreciated was his courage.

It inspired her.

She would need it for this.

She changed into her gown and placed her belongings inside a tiny, narrow steel locker.

It reminded her of a vertical coffin.

Would she soon be inside a coffin too?

She pulled the rubber key chain around her wrist.

"Number 101. Maybe that's my lucky number." She sat and waited. But not for long.

"Miss Martinez. We're ready for you."

She climbed on top of a gurney as they wheeled her into the cold sterilized operating room.

Surrounded by masked nurses, an anesthesiologist, and other

assorted medical staff.

All this for me? wondered Emily as she tried to calm herself.

"Your hand is freezing!" one of them said. "There's nothing to worry about. Just lie still. It'll be over before you know it!"

They wrapped her tightly in heated blankets like a newborn baby.

"We'll start the anesthesia as soon as the doctor gets here, ok?" She would welcome the sleep, as she hadn't been getting any rest for the last few weeks.

"Here he is!"

Someone turned on some music.

Rock and roll.

She liked it. But wondered whether it might be too distracting for Dr. Wu.

After all, she didn't want him to make any mistakes.

"Good morning, Emily. You ok?"

She nodded and felt a tear run down her cheek.

"Don't cry, Emily. It's going to be alright. I promise you." He felt his heart break just a bit.

It was the first time that one of them ever cried on his operating table.

"You ok?"

She nodded and closed her eyes, wanting it to be over already.

"I'll be right back ok.? They're going to give you the anesthesia now, ok? I'll be right back."

A rubbery mask was placed over her mouth and nose. "Hi, I'm Dr. Lawrence. I'll be monitoring you today. Just take deep breaths."

She began to inhale as she tried to stay awake.

She caught a glimpse of Dr. Wu.

Right outside the room.

His head bowed.

It looked as if he was praying!

"That's it. Good girl. Deep breaths!"

In what felt like seconds she heard a voice summoning her back to consciousness.

"Emily! Emily! Wake up! Can you hear me! Emily?"

"What?"

"Emily, you like this music? What's your favorite music?" She heard Dr. Wu and remembered the music before she went under.

She remembered where she was.

The surgery was over.

"Yes, I like rock and roll but not this group though!"

It made him laugh.

She wanted to laugh too.

It was finally over.

"We're taking you over to the recovery room. Then we'll take you to your room, ok, Emily? You did a great job, Emily! Good job!"

"Okay. Thanks, Dr. Wu."

He looked tired.

Really, really tired.

"We'll be right here if you need us. It'll take a while for the anesthesia to wear off."

She wanted to sleep, but wanted to stay awake.

To stay alive.

They covered her with more blankets.

"You're going to feel some pain soon, Emily, from the surgery. It will be very painful. But we'll give you something for that, ok?"

That's right.

Major surgery.

Dr. Wu had no other choice.

But she didn't feel anything.

She felt the same.

But she knew she was different.

Uterus-less.

No hope of ever having any children now.

"Just relax and we'll be right back, ok?"

She wanted to run.

Run out of there as fast as possible.

Back to her normal life.

Far away from cancer.

She wondered if she'd ever be able to run ever again.

She'll ask him about it later.

But now, she was tired.

She gave into the sleep.

Luis was the first to get up from the couch in the waiting area. Her brother was there along with her mom and older sister. "Damn, Dr. Wu, that was a long time," complained Luis. "You said that it would only take a few hours. It's been nearly eight!" Dr. Wu knew that his guy was a hothead, but he appreciated his concern for Emily's well being.

"Listen, please…it was worse than I thought…."

He saw it in their eyes immediately.

The panic, fear and profound sadness.

"It spread…"

Those awful words.

How many more times would he have to say it to other

families?

"She's gonna need chemo and maybe radiation. The cancer broke through the uterus and into the lining of the stomach."

The family remained silent.

Shock always does that.

"I'll do my best to help her, but it's not good. I had to remove everything. All of her reproductive organs. I'm sorry."

Luis' cell phone rang.

"Listen, man I gotta call you back," Luis said as he ended the call.

"Please don't say anything to her yet, ok, Dr. Wu? Please let her get through this, and then later we'll tell her, ok?"

He actually liked this guy, despite his jealousy. "Sure. Sure. That's a good idea. Listen, I gotta get back to the office. Emily will stay here for a few days. Then we'll start the chemo. Don't worry. We'll get through this, ok?"

He shook hands with everyone, including the mother. A small, Puerto Rican woman. So fragile. He felt her fear. "I'll do my best to help your daughter, Mrs. Martinez." That's what he'd promise to all the parents.

"Goodbye for now."

He walked away from them feeling their eyes upon his back.

Damn it!

He was just a doctor and a surgeon.

He wasn't God!

He walked past his assistant's desk.

"No calls, Carmen."

He was in desperate need of a drink.

And some companionship.

"Hi, Tanya. It's Dr. Wu."

He would always insist that his girlfriends called him Dr. Wu.

He was never on a first name basis with anyone.

"I'll pick you up in an hour."

He liked Tanya.

Cute, young, and good in bed.

A nurse from Mount Sinai.

But there was nothing more there, and thank goodness, they both knew it.

He sat and opened her chart.

How could he describe what it was that he saw today in the OR?

He fingered the ballpoint pen, clinking it several times.

"Emily Martinez, age 39. Surgical patient. 8 hour long surgery…complex case."

But what about the light that he saw? From the very first cut into her soft flesh…

"Do you see that?"

The oncological nurse handed him the cotton gauze to control the bleeding.

"What?"

He continued with the incision.

From the base of her vagina up and around her belly button.

A bikini cut.

Makes the scar less noticeable.

But with each cut, the light poured out from her and became more and more radiant--nearly filling the room with its blinding beam. "Don't you see that?"

The nurse knew of his demanding schedules and his devotion to his saving his patients.

"Maybe we should call Dr. Montijo…he might be available…"

He had to shake it off. Ignore it.

No one else saw what he saw.

He had to keep his hands steady.

He had to continue.

"I'm fine! Must be my eyes playing tricks on me!"

But he knew what he saw as her light saturated the small room; an internal flashlight for him, as it guided him to every single tiny cancer cell, making sure that he would remove every single last one.

He was convinced that he was now performing surgery on one of God's truest messengers.

He knew that he would never again meet anyone like her.

The hours flew as he continued.

"Let's do the final wash. Make sure that we got everything."

He saw that it had metastasized.

"She's toast."

But he got every last bit of it.

He had to save her. His life depended on it.

"Come on. Let's close her up. She's got a long road ahead of her."

He returned to his chart.

He closed the folder.

He would keep the light a secret.

One day, when he was John, and not Dr. Wu, and she was Emily, and not his patient, he would tell her of the miracle inside her, and how it made him love her.

***

They had to start the treatment as soon as possible.

The nurse walked in with the IV for the first round of chemo drugs.

"We will do this intravenously until they insert a catheter."

Emily tried to sit up. The pain was excruciating.

"It hurts, huh?"

"Yeah, it hurts."

"Push the button for the morphine. That's what it's there for."

"No, it's okay. I don't like it."

"You're in pain. You just had major surgery. Punch the damn button! You're gonna need it!" Emily succumbed.

"That's better. Today we start with this one. In a few hours we'll start the second one, and then tomorrow the last one, ok?"

Three different chemo drugs. She was really sick.

"Okay."

She remembered that Dr. Wu came by last night to check up on her.

She was surprised by the late night visit. But she was happy to see him.

"So, here's the deal, my dear."

He called her dear.

That's funny.

She liked it.

"It's a little bit worse than we thought, Emily."

She knew what was coming.

She felt it.

"Listen. It's Stage Four. That's not so good. Stage one, stage two or sometimes even stage three, we can make it better."

She held her breath, not wanting to inhale for fear of not hearing what he had to tell her.

"Listen, Emily, your chances for survival are zero to 8%. You understand?"

Yeah, she understood.

Zero to 8%.

Maybe she'll be in the 8%.

"But we're gonna do all we can to make sure you're ok, ok?"

"Sure, Dr. Wu. But I have one question."

He knew what was coming.

The tears, the horror, the prayers.

"I just want to know one thing…will I still be able to run?"

"Run?"

"Yes, run. I'm a runner. I like to run. I just wanna know if I can still run."

She had one thing going for her…optimism.

"My dear, if you can still run, after all of the drugs that I'm gonna give you, that in itself will be a miracle!"

She felt a little relief---happy to know that she would not lose her ability to feel free.

"Okay. Thanks, Dr. Wu."

She settled back into her pain, as the nurse began to administer the first chemo drug.

It was time to take control.

It was time to make it into the 8%.

That night, he laid in his bed and thought of her again.

Knowing that she'd lose all of her hair soon saddened him.

He walked to his dresser's mirror.

"I could use a haircut as well."

He thought she might like that.

A show of solidarity and empathy.

He noticed the paunch that he had grown in the last few months.

"I think I should lose some weight. She'll like that too. And these…"

He stopped himself.

He walked into the kitchen and found himself a beer.

He had to keep it all under wraps.

But that light inside her.

That mysterious light.

She was different.

Very special.

He turned on the television, and searched for a stupid, mindless movie.

It would keep his mind off of her.

At least for some time.

Until after she was no longer his patient.

When he would be free to love her.

***

The six months of treatment came and went, as did Luis.

Her refusal to have sex with him was based on how painful it was when they tried so soon after her surgery.

No more sex, no more Luis.

She told Dr. Wu about it when she met him at the clinic.

"Sorry about that Emily. Sorry that he's not around to hear the good news."

"What good news?"

"The results from last week's blood work came in. It's gone, Emily. The cancer is all gone. You're in remission! There won't be any need for radiation. We can stop the chemo now."

Was it true?

Had it really gone away?

"Your hair will grow back, Emily. Maybe almost as beautiful as it was before."

Oh, damn!

He slipped!

"I mean, the way that it was before."

Emily removed her baseball cap, her hair all gone, that she wore nearly all the time except when she slept.

"And the catheter?"

He explained how they would monitor her for five years before declaring her as completely cured.

"Just another year with the catheter, Emily. After that we can remove it. But we'll continue to monitor you for three more years after that, ok?"

His talk of the future brightened her outlook.

She would still be around for at least another five more years!

"Let's see you in two weeks, ok?"

In the months and years that followed, he kept his feelings for her to himself.

Never slipping. Not once.

But soon he would be able to tell her.

Soon he would be ready to love her.

"Everything looks good Emily. It's been in remission for five years now. You're cured! You're in that 8%!"

Her hair was almost down to her shoulders.

It grew back differently though.

Not as thick as before.

But still curly and dark.

"Cured? Really?"

She leaned back against the tall chemo chairs.

She wanted to hug him but knew that she couldn't.

Over time, she had developed feelings for him.

She could tell that he liked her too. "So, that means we can celebrate?" His heart stopped.

"Celebrate?"

"Well, you remember Sonia?" Yes. Stage Two Ovarian.

She didn't make it.

"Before she passed, she told me to have a bottle of champagne with you when I was cured. I want to honor that." He wanted to kiss her right there and then.

"Of course. It's a date."

Emily had already made a reservation, weeks ago, at her favorite restaurant in Long Island City, in anticipation of this very moment. It was on the water, and it served the best seafood in town.

She knew that Dr. Wu would like it.

"Great! Then it's a date, Dr. Wu."

"Please call me John."

The waiter showed her to their table as he pulled out the chair for her.

"Would you like something to drink while you're waiting?"

"Yes. Champagne, please."

As she waited for Dr. Wu, she thought about him, and what she would reveal to him that evening.

How much she appreciated how he was always there for her. Even those late-night calls that he'd take after another marathon of vomiting. After losing her hair. After losing Luis. After the neuropathy started in her toes. After the pain that she felt in her bones from the chemo drugs. After the fatigue. After the worry. After all of it. He was always there.

She treasured it.

She wanted to thank him. For saving her life, and caring for her.

She wanted to tell him what she felt in her heart for him.

How it grew into love over the years.

Finally!

She would say something.

She was no longer his patient.

She would be free to speak of her love for him.

What she couldn't tell him as his patient.

What she could now tell him as a woman.

 "I brought two glasses."

The waiter poured the beverage filling her glass to the top.

"Thank you. My date should be here soon."

She raised her glass and thought of Sonia, and the others that she met and got to know, who were no longer with her.

"This is for you, my friends," said Emily as she poured a bit of the liquid onto the bare floor. "I miss you."

He had been preparing for their date together for five years. Ever since that morning when he first saw her in his office. He rushed through his appointments for the day. Thankful that he did not have too many patients to see, he was able to leave the office a little early.

He adjusted his tie and the new designer jacket that he just bought especially for the occasion.

Of course, the dinner would be his treat. He would never

allow her to pay.

He would always make sure that she was happy from now on and for the rest of her life.

From now on, it would be them.

From now on, it will be John and Emily. Just them.

He fell in love with her fearlessness as she faced a supposed death, and he knew that she was the one, perhaps even without witnessing her extraordinary light. But her light cemented his love for her forever.

"*Finally*, I will tell her what's been in my heart all these years."

Dr. Wu hurried to his parked BMW.

He looked at his watch as he started the car.

It was only a twenty-minute ride to the restaurant from where he lived.

"She's probably already there…"

The car came out of nowhere; colliding into the driver's side where he sat, sending his car into a lamppost, head first. In an instant he saw his departed grandfather Xiang in Taiwan preparing some soup.

"If you want to become a surgeon, young man, you must eat all of your broth. It will make you skillful and provide you with the acumen that you will need." Dr. Wu looked to his right.

His grandfather was now seated beside him in the shattered vehicle.

"You don't have to worry about your patients, John. They will be taken care of."

He thought of Emily, waiting for him at the restaurant.

Waiting for their love to begin.

He wanted to weep.

"I'm sorry, Emily. I did my best."

His grandfather's touch was gentle.

"It's time to come with me, young man."

"Yes, Baba."

Dr. Wu reached his hand through the wreckage and saw the light, the one once inside her, now resembling millions of tiny sparkly dots, that covered the spiritual orb, his new home, as he took two of the stars and placed one in each eye, promising to her that he would be her beacon and perpetually watch over his truest love.

Emily looked at the large, round decorative clock that hung on the wall opposite their table.

"Maybe he won't come."

The waiter tried to take the extra glass away.

"No, please. Leave it there, please…"

He politely nodded his head.

"Of course…"

She felt it but didn't dare say it.

She filled his glass with the champagne.

"He's already here…with me…"

Emily clinked her glass with his as its muted chime echoed in her core. "Thank you, Dr. Wu."

THE ERASABLE MAN

Bobby Jose Iglesias was a handsome, young Black man with high, chiseled cheekbones and lustrous tobacco skin. He was so beautiful that his friends and family nicknamed him "negrito." Bobby was flattered by the endearment. It was only his skin color that made life so difficult. Or so he thought.

Bobby always kept his appearance well-groomed and presentable and wore his soft, curly afro underneath a New York Yankees baseball cap. Some say that he resembled Roberto Clemente, the late, Puerto Rican, major league baseball player who was killed in a plane crash while on his way to Nicaragua to help the survivors of an earthquake. The comparison both honored and distressed Bobby who knew of the vicious racism hurled at Clemente throughout his life, despite his noble efforts on and off the field.

Bobby worked nights at an all-night Duane Reade pharmacy in downtown Manhattan. He didn't mind the graveyard shift because at least, with so few customers, it gave him the extra time and solitude in which to study. And besides, it paid well, at least a few more dollars than minimum wage so that he could pay for his pre-med studies at the city university where the tuition had gone up again this year. Whatever money was left over he would give to his maternal aunt, Carmen, a glowing, moon face, heavy-set black woman with ruddy cheeks and a generous soul, who he lived with in a two-bedroom apartment in Inwood since the age of two.

"You were the cutest little negrito that I ever saw Bobby!" she would often exclaim with a gap-toothed appreciation. "Exactamente como tu mama, hijo!"

Indeed, Bobby did resemble his mother Alicia, a dark-haired Cuban beauty, with eyes of canela and deep cocoa skin. But his father's departure proved too much to bear for the young mother, who Titi Carmen explained, one day disappeared, leaving her sister, Carmen, to care for the small child.

"She did not even leave a note, mi'jo. God only knows where she is!"

Sherman Avenue in Inwood was where Bobby called home and where he would race to once he was done with his late-night shift at the store. At the pharmacy, Bobby would help out with anything, whether it was doing inventory, stocking shelves, or working at the register.

As long as he got paid, he didn't mind.

It was already past midnight. Bobby had to take over the register because Maddie called in sick again. Maddie was his best friend whose only concern in life was having fun, at least for now, since she was only seventeen. Maddie lived with her dad on West 161st and St. Nick, along with her two younger sisters. Maddie dropped out of school because she found it too boring and found better companionship with the books in the public library.

Maddie was one of those natural geniuses and intended to return to school, and maybe get her GED and apply at one of the city colleges. But first, she wanted to use her youth and energy on the more important things in her life right now, making money and spending it. All of the money that she earned at the pharmacy was enough to pay for new clothes, help out at home, and go to the clubs downtown, even if she was still underage.

But he was worried. She had been calling in sick a lot or showing up late. He feared that Maddie was losing interest in her all-important job since it was all that she had going for her right now and jobs, right now, were too scarce to throw away.

"That'll be $15.95."

The economy was getting worse. Why just the other day, Mr. Jenkins, his boss, had to raise the price of a 100-count bottle of Tylenol by a dollar. Bobby would wait patiently as customers dug deeper into their purses for the once carelessly tossed aside loose change, now used to purchase their much needed items.

And this customer was no different as she fished through her coin purse, handing the quarters and dimes and nickels to Bobby, closing her purse with a loud snap that punctuated the pain of the purchase.

"These prices are too high! I can't even afford to have a headache anymore!"

Bobby wished that he could give it all away for free when he saw how hard people worked to make ends meet, even in this part of town, where the rents were much more expensive than where he lived with Titi Carmen.

"Here's your change, miss."

As he placed the change in her hand Bobby noticed how she reacted; how the white fingers would always pull back from his, avoiding the slightest touch, which was hard to do when he tried to return their change.

"Thank you."

She didn't even try to hide her bigotry.

"Where's the girl?"

Bobby was no idiot. Maddie was a light-skin Latina and could easily pass for white. It killed him, each slight, each dismissal, verbal and otherwise. They didn't even know him and didn't even care to know him; a hard-working college honors student who helped out his aunt at home. Couldn't they see that?

Couldn't they see beyond the color?

"You mean Maddie? The white girl?"

He couldn't help it, it just slipped out. He was tired. It was a long day. He longed for his bed.

"Yeah, her. Where is she?"

Bobby was amazed at how she could not even detect his bitterness and his humanness.

"She's sick. Next!"

As he finished with the last customer Bobby began to tidy up the area that Maddie had turned into a makeshift workstation for herself near one of the registers. He saw the picture of Maddie with her two younger sisters. Bobby respected how hard she worked to care for them since their moms passed.

Bobby stared lovingly at the pretty girl in the photo—at her luxurious wavy-curly hair, the same color of those chestnuts that they sell in those little street carts downtown around Christmas time, milk chocolate eyes and a kind face that made you feel loved; he had a big-time crush on Maddie, although she once made it clear that they were only friends.

"Bobby!"

Mr. Jenkins approached him and spoke with a tone that

meant business.

"One of the customers, Bobby…"

Bobby watched as the racist woman exited the store looking back slightly to make sure that indeed the deed was done.

"She said that you were rude. We can't have any of that stuff here, Bobby. If it happens again, I'm gonna have to let you go. You understand?"

Bobby slid closed the register's drawer as it sang a small *ting*.

"Yes, sir. The customer is always right."

"That's right. Now get back to work! Some supplies came in and I need them to be ticketed."

"Yes, sir."

Bobby liked Mr. Jenkins. He was a short, stocky man, who worked at the drugstore since it opened over thirty years ago. He, like Bobby, earned his way through school and later became a pharmacist and has never worked anywhere else since. Bobby admired Mr. Jenkins, and even considered him a father figure, who he would always speak to whenever he needed advice like when the customers treated him like he was toxic or when he couldn't hail down a cab in that part of town, late at night, and would wind up taking the long A train ride home. Mr. Jenkins was cool, even for a white guy.

"Listen, Bobby, you can't let that stuff bother you, son. You gotta just let it all roll off your back. Look at me!" Mr. Jenkins gently pulled on the lapels of his white lab coat with great satisfaction. "I'm still here despite all the crap that I get from the owner about profit and overhead and such and I don't let it get to me. And those customers! Ha!" He patted his balding head and frowned. "Sometimes even I can't stand them! I just don't let it get under my skin, Bobby, and you can't let it get under yours!"

But to Bobby that was the problem and the root of his troubles; it was all about his skin and its color. Bobby would always listen to Mr. Jenkins with great respect, but he just didn't get it. He would never be able to understand.

"Sure thing, Mr. Jenkins. Just let it roll off my back."

"You're a good kid, Bobby. Let's get back to work."

Bobby locked the register and wandered to Aisle 6 where he found a multitude of sealed, unpriced boxes of merchandise. He ripped open one of the boxes marked "spiral notebooks," and made a mental note to buy one for his bio-chem class.

"What's this?"

The box was one that Bobby had never seen before.

Magic Pencils

Bobby opened the box and found several boxes inside it. "Must be for the kiddies," he surmised as he handled one of the boxes with great care.

Bobby removed the item from the box, a row of 36 brightly colored sticks, all neatly assembled inside a clear, zippered plastic bag.

Bobby dramatically waved one of the pencils, a red one, in the air like a wand. "Abracadabra!" Bobby scanned the store not wanting Mr. Jenkins to appear out of thin air to accuse him of goofing off.

"Cute pencil, but not magic!" he concluded.

Bobby was just about to return it into its bag when he noticed its unusually large eraser. It was one that he had never seen before on any pencil. It seemed to be more of a sponge.

Bobby took one of the notebooks and printed his name on one of the sheets.

"Writes like a normal pencil," he observed as he admired his name on the ruled page.

Bobby began to erase his name from the sheet but as hard as he tried, it would not disappear.

"I gotta tell Mr. Jenkins to return these," thought Bobby, hoping that maybe he could score some points with Mr. J after what occurred with that white lady.

Once again, Bobby worked to expunge his name. "Man, I hope he can get a refund. This eraser is crap!"

Bobby put the now used notebook away, promising to purchase it, as he began to write his mother's name on his brown palm: *Alicia.*

"Bobby! I need you on the register!"

Bobby hurried to wipe off the name. "Shit! I can't get this off!"

"Bobby! I need you A-S-A-P!"

Bobby continued to apply more pressure on his hand with the pencil's eraser but her name remained, still intact, as his name did in the notebook.

"Come on, come on, get off, get off!!" he yelled uncontrollably, not fully understanding what was happening.

Soon the pencil's eraser began to remove not only the red print in his palm but his own color as well!

"What the fuck is this?" he said as he stared at his hand with absolute disbelief.

"Nah, man this is crazy! I need help!" he shrieked as he violently threw the pencil down the aisle and glared at the large, white spot on his palm. "I need help! Oh, my God! What did I do?"

"Bobby! I need you now! Up front!"

Bobby raced down the aisle with the rest of the pencils, stopping to lock them safely inside one of the storage cabinets beneath the display area to keep them away from nosy customers just until he could speak to Mr. Jenkins or Maddie about what happened.

"Bobby!"

"I'm coming, Mr. Jenkins!"

Bobby told himself that as soon as he had a moment, he would wash with some of the antibacterial soap in the employees' restroom.

"You're too late, Bobby! Didn't you hear me?"

Bobby stood by his side as he stared down hard at the closed cash register, embarrassed and wounded by the man's admonishment and worried about his hand.

"There you go, Miss. Have a nice evening." Mr. Jenkins turned towards Bobby as the woman exited the store. "Bobby, what am I going to do with you? What were you doing out there? I told you to put away the stationery supplies, not take an inventory of the entire store!"

"Sorry, Mr. Jenkins, it's just those pencils…you know, the magical ones that you ordered…"

Mr. Jenkins crossed from behind the counter as he fiddled with the candy display. "Now what are you talking about Bobby? What magical pencils? We don't carry any magic stuff. Maybe during Halloween, but never any magic pencils. Where are those jumbo size Milk Duds?"

Bobby stretched his arm over the counter and pointed towards the corner.

"We keep them over here, Mr. J."

"We're running low. I better get some more from the back. Stay here until we close. Your shift is almost over anyway."

"Wait, Mr. Jenkins! Wait! It's my hand! Look! Look!"

Mr. Jenkins closely examined the discoloration as if he were a real doctor. "How did this happen?"

"I told you! It's those pencils, Mr. J. I wrote my mother's name on my palm and tried to erase it, but this happened instead. What is it, Mr. J? What is it?"

"Now settle down, Bobby!

Mr. Jenkins wiped the area several times with his index finger.

"It's nothing, Bobby. Maybe there's just some bleach in the eraser. A factory flaw. It'll go away in a few days. Don't worry! It's not like you're disappearing!"

Bobby was still unconvinced that it was just bleach.

"And next time, Bobby, please come when you're called. Lucky for me none of the customers complained about the wait or else we would have had a lot of unhappy people here, Bobby, including me, understand?"

Of course, he understood the veiled threat. Bobby needed this job more than anything. He could not rely on his aunt anymore, especially after they cut back on her hours at the place where she cleans offices. To lose this job would mean to lose his future and that was something that he could not afford to do.

That night, at home, after finishing his assignments and

taking a long shower, Bobby noticed that despite the hot water and the Ivory Soap, he still could not remove the colorless area.

It *was* magic!

Deep down in his heart, something told him that something or perhaps even someone, wanted him to find that box and use those pencils. It was his fate.

Bobby crawled into bed and began to think of the day, the entire day, going over all of the scenes and images that played out; about Maddie and worrying if she was all right; about Mr. J. and how angry he was at him; he thought about his Titi, now sleeping soundly in her room, after ending her shift, and how he adored her; and he thought about his mother and when he was reminded, how similar he was to her, as black as a cup of Bustelo espresso coffee, and wondered where she was.

He wondered if somehow it was she who wanted him to find that box, but that was too strange to think, as he thought about his life as a young, black, Hispanic man, in the city, and how he had to take the long train ride home yet again that night because a taxi would not stop for him.

And then he thought about that box again, filled with the enchanted instruments that could erase his blackness with such ease, and change him into a color that would make his life easier; by not having to wait forever to hail a cab and without white ladies cringing when he would return their change.

But that was impossible to even imagine, he thought, as the sleep overwhelmed him and he silently wished for a peaceful dream.

***

Maddie was just about done with her shift at the pharmacy as she waited anxiously for Bobby to arrive.

"Maddie, count your register before you leave. You forgot to do it the other day."

"Si, Señor Jenkins," she said with a deliberate accent.

"Just do as I say, Maddie, no jokes, ok?"

"Yes, Mr. Jenkins."

Maddie was growing tired of doing the same shit, day in and day out. She made a huge mistake by dropping out in her senior year, being an honors student and all, but she wanted to experience life, real life, but now, she hated it. Although she didn't mind the extra cash, she just couldn't stand the constant repetition of the job. At least while she was in school, she was in a different class every day and got to see her friends.

This life, even if it was real, was truly boring, intellectually speaking. Thank God for her books at the library.

Maddie stared up at the clock, happy to know that Bobby would soon be there. She could finally tell him her great news and the reason she had been calling in sick. "He's gonna be happier than flies on shit!" she cheerfully proclaimed as she put on her navy blue Duane Reade work smock.

Maddie was dying for a cigarette. She placed her KOOLs in her pocket remembering to grab a book of matches for later.

Bobby entered just as she reached the door to the store's locker room.

"Hey, Maddie! Are you feeling better?"

"Yo, bro, you'll never guess what happened to me. Guess! Guess!"

"I don't know Maddie. I'm not good at guessing. Are you pregnant?"

Maddie pulled him into the staff lounge and lit her cigarette.

"Is that all you think about me? Shoot!"

She inhaled deeply, allowing the menthol to cool her simmering thoughts.

"I thought you liked me, Bobby!"

Of course, he liked her, more than anyone in the world, besides his Titi Carmen.

"I was joking, can't you take a joke?"

Bobby gazed at his palm; still void of its true color.

"I got something to tell you too, Maddie. Something weird."

Maddie pulled him towards the small round table that always rocked. She placed her book of matches under one of the legs to steady it.

"I'm going back to school, bro! That's why I had to take those days off. I went back to my high school and Mrs. Norman, my guidance counselor, said that since I was an honors student it would only take a couple of months to make up for the courses that I never completed and then she's gonna help me apply for college, bro. College! And guess what, bro? She told me that I could have been class valedictorian if I had stayed in school, man, and that she would try to help me get into one of the Ivy League schools. Ain't that cool, bro? Ain't that great?"

Bobby was happy for her, but the mere mention of "Ivy League" sent a groan through his body. He could have also applied, but he only averaged a B and that was not enough to get into any of those schools, even with his perfect SATs score.

Besides, he could never afford it, even with student loans. It would be too much to ask from his Titi and to ask of himself. "Wow! That's great Maddie, but those schools are expensive. How you gonna pay for that?"

"Mrs. Norman said that she's gonna try to help me get a full scholarship. Good thing that I'm not only smart but I'm also broke ass poor!"

"I'm proud of you, Maddie. We gotta celebrate later, ok?" Bobby turned to exit the small lounge.

"But what about you, bro? What's your news? Maybe we can have a double celebration!"

Bobby remembered what Mr. Jenkins said about the bleach and how that might have caused the problem.

"Nothing like yours, Maddie. Just something that I found in Aisle 6, in stationery." Bobby gave her his hand. He liked how she held it, how it made him feel less afraid and calm all at once.

"What the fuck is this, man? Did you get into some of those hair removal products in Aisle 3? You gotta be careful, bro…that's some strong shit, and it stinks too, like rotten eggs!"

Bobby pulled away from her.

"No, Maddie. I found this weird little box and it was marked 'magic pencils' and then I opened it and tried it out. Like, I wrote my mother's name right here, and then I began to erase it, 'cause Mr. Jenkins needed me up front and this is what happened. I started changing color."

Maddie laughed and lit a cigarette. The inhaled smoke

pushed out of her nose and mouth at the same time, like a crooked chimney.

"That's crazy, man! Change your color? Pencils that could change your color?! Oh, like if I was green and I wanted to be blue? Crazy!"

Bobby turned his back to her and left the room.

"When you're done with your cig, Maddie, meet me in aisle 6 and I'll show you."

Maddie stomped out her KOOL into the cheap tin ashtray already filled with discarded gum wrappers and gray balls of Wrigley's spearmint gum.

"He's nuts!" she muttered as she followed him down the corridor.

"Yo, Maddie, Come here! You gotta see this! Give me your arm!"

"Hey! What the fuck are you doing?"

"Shh! Just watch."

Bobby persisted as he continued to move the pencil's spongy tip on her forearm.

"Nothing's happening. Maybe there's something wrong with it. Let me try another one."

But as much as he tried, Maddie's light summer tan remained the same.

"Maybe it was just that one, Bobby, the one that you used yesterday. Maybe there was something in it, like a chemical or something, like it was defective or something and that's what made you like that."

"Here. Let me try it again on me." With little effort, Bobby, once again, removed more of his color. "See! I told you!"

"You're getting white!"

Bobby craned his neck to see that Mr. Jenkins wasn't coming back any time soon. By this time his palm was completely white.

"Bobby! That's fucked up!" Maddie grabbed the pencil away from Bobby and shoved it back inside the box.

"You better stop that! It's poison! You don't know what kinda shit is in that shit!" she continued. "You better hide that fucking box or put it away somewhere. Come on, we better get to the front. Mr. Jenkins is almost done with the prescriptions."

Maddie sped to the register as Bobby stayed behind, searching for another hiding place.

"I'll just take them home with me," Bobby decided. "I'll let Mr. J. know tomorrow. I'm sure he won't mind."

As he walked towards Maddie, Bobby found it odd that it didn't work on her.

And he remembered his thoughts from the night before and was convinced that they were for him.

As he recalled these thoughts, he was certain that by tomorrow he would become a new man.

When his shift was over, and Maddie had already gone home, Bobby took his usual route to the train. But, since it was so late, he decided to try to flag down a taxi for the ride home.

Titi always gave him extra money for a cab for late nights like this one.

"Yo, kid!"

The police car came out of nowhere, furtively snaking its way towards Bobby, as the cop in the passenger seat spoke to him through the open window.

"Let's see some fucking ID!"

Bobby was familiar with these late night drills.

Just stay calm, be respectful and never, ever talk back.

"Yes, officer."

The police car stopped as the two tall men walked out of the vehicle and brandished their guns.

"Up against the wall."

One of the cops, a white guy, violently pulled off Bobby's backpack to search it as the other, a black cop, patted him down.

"Where you from? Why are you here? What are you up to at this time of night? Where do you live?"

Before he could answer, the cop unzipped his bag and dumped its contents onto the sidewalk, unconcerned that Bobby paid $200 for one of the chemistry books that now lay split open in two, soiled by the dirty concrete.

"There's just books here, no contraband."

The cop noticed the small box on the ground, pointing it out to Bobby with his stout chin. "What the fuck is that?"

The other cop stopped frisking Bobby, finding only his wallet that contained the twenty dollars from his aunt and a MetroCard. "This kid's clean, man, maybe we should let him go."

The white cop forcefully pulled Bobby down towards the sidewalk by the sleeves of his hoodie, dragging him close to the pavement, the tip of his nose smelling the city's filth. "I said, what's in the box, kid?"

Bobby's heart raced as he wondered what would come next. "Just some pencils, Officer, that I bought for school.

Here…I'll show you."

Bobby reached down to retrieve the container but was stopped with a stinging rap to his knees. "Get the fuck back! You move too fast, kid!"

Bobby wanted to yell out in pain but dared not to.

"Nice and slow, kid," the black cop advised. "You make any sudden moves and you make my partner here nervous, entiendes?"

Bobby nodded "yes" as he moved towards the box, opening it as if it were glass. "It's just pencils, see?"

The white cop grabbed the box, looked inside and then threw it back on the sidewalk. "Pick up your shit and get the fuck outta here! Don't let me see you around here again. Stay in your own fucking neighborhood! Next time, we might not be so nice."

Bobby wanted to tell them that he couldn't stay in his own neighborhood where there were no jobs, that he worked at the Duane Reade just around the block and how he needed to work to stay in school, but why would they care about any of that?

"Yes, Officer."

Bobby wanted to cry but didn't as he picked up his books and the box and prayed that the officers would not change their minds about letting him go, and take him somewhere dark and hidden, in an alley somewhere, where they would really beat the crap outta him, and no one would ever find him again, or ever know what happened or even give it a second thought because he was black and they were cops.

"Fucking kids…"

The cop's words trailed off as they entered the squad car

and quietly drove away.

Bobby pulled his backpack up, over, and around his shoulders as he changed his mind about the cab and headed towards the nearest subway.

***

His Titi was already asleep and had thoughtfully left him some roasted chicken and a plate of arroz con gandules for him to heat up when he arrived, but Bobby wasn't hungry. He was mad.

Bobby tore off his clothes and jumped into the shower. He vowed that he would never allow that to ever happen again to him. He promised that from now on he would travel anywhere in the city, as he pleased, wherever and whenever he wished, without fear or anxiety about what might happen, and he stepped out of the tub, assured of the miracle contained in the box, which would beget his freedom.

Bobby moved to his bed and counted the pencils. He would need to use them all to fulfill his goal.

And thus began the transformation, into the night and into the next morning, using each one, until he could erase no more, until he was completely rid of himself, rid of pain, his disappointment and the intense burden that he carried.

Bobby walked to the mirror on his dresser, naked and white.

He stared at the white man that he had become.

Now he would be safe.

Bobby, exhausted and sore from the exhilarating makeover, stumbled into his bed and fell into a deep sleep.

Bobby awoke hours later.

Was it all a dream?

He approached the mirror. "Whoa! I am white!" he announced excitedly as he clumsily pirouetted in the air. "I'm white…and it wasn't a dream!"

Instantly, he thought about his Titi. How would she react? What would she do or say? But he didn't care. Things would be different for him from now on as he hurried to prepare himself for what was left of the rest of the day.

"Maddie's not going to believe this!" he whispered as he searched his closet and wondered what in the world he would wear as a white man.

He immediately noticed how others reacted, the subtle differences, as he walked through his neighborhood towards the downtown subway. He noticed how they stared at him, a young white man, a stranger to their browner surroundings.

Bobby stopped at the corner donut shop where he would usually get his coffee and buttered roll. Two cops were standing near its entrance, not the ones from last night, but the same. Bobby held his breath and waited for the assault.

"Here you go, son!"

The cop held the door open for the handsome, young, white man.

"Thank you, Officer!" Bobby's enthused response betrayed his inner joy as he moved towards the counter.

"What can I get for you, sir?" The guy at the counter immediately went to help him, ignoring the other men and women, shades darker than he, who were waiting to be served.

And the guy was polite, real polite, not like how he would speak to Bobby, like in the past.

"Here you go, sir. Have a lovely day!" Bobby could feel the tension from the other customers seeping into his paler skin, but he didn't care. It wasn't his fault that the counter guy tended to him first, right?

Bobby walked with his sweetened coffee feeling lighter and whiter with each step.

He stopped at the newsstand to buy his regular copy of the *New York Daily News* as he did every day. He spotted a copy of that month's *Time* magazine to skim through.

"Take your time, sir. That's a good magazine."

Bobby was startled by the hospitality. Normally the vendor would chase him out for not buying the magazine.

Bobby flipped through the magazine not really reading it at all but taking in the luxury of being allowed to touch it and read it, and not have to buy it, now as a white man. From now on he wouldn't be shooed away like some annoying little shit-fly. He could stay there all day and read the entire magazine if he wanted to.

"Come back again, sir!"

Bobby noticed the others, waiting to pay for their newspapers, rolling their eyes at him, knowing that he had been pushed ahead of them, knowing that they would always come second.

But as he turned to leave, Bobby felt a scorching hiss enter his left ear.

"Pendejo, whitey! Think they own the fucking world!"

Bobby stopped in his tracks. He recognized the voice coming from a familiar face from his neighborhood, someone who would always say hello to him, and he would always say hello back to as well. She didn't know him anymore.

He walked away now, a puzzled white man, feeling the same as when the cops stopped him the night before when he was black.

At school some of his teachers noticed a change while others really didn't bother or were too polite to inquire. In the large city university, where so many came and went, students' faces were just a blur.

But Bobby continued to notice the difference. How the security guards allowed him to pass throughout the school without even checking his ID like before.

Bobby wandered into the cafeteria to waste time and found a table near the windows where the light was good, and the sun could warm his white arms. A young woman, pretty with blonde hair approached him.

"Mind if I sit here? My name's April. I'm a bio-chem major. Aren't you in one of my labs?"

Bobby never thought of introducing himself before. Yes, they were in the same class, but she always seemed too busy with her friends to bother with him.

"Yeah, I'm Bobby…"

"Bobby?"

He remembered now that he was different. How he had changed. "I mean Robert. You can call me Bob."

The two chatted for a while as Bobby noticed the other students around them. The subtle division. The separation was so obvious. Black and White. Now he saw everything so clearly. And this deeply troubled him.

Throughout the rest of the day, Bobby became aware that things had not really changed for him and came to grips with the fact that life was not different at all but was really the same.

Later that day, Bobby noticed Maddie at the register as he entered the store and waited in line, behind a customer, to greet her.

"Yes, may I help you sir?"

Maddie didn't look at him straight in the eye, like she always did, but off to the side with her eyes half-closed, a polite acquiescence, as he would do when he spoke to the white customers in the past.

"Maddie!"

"Yes? How do you know my name?"

Bobby wanted to run away, jump right out of his new white skin, saddened that his friend, his only friend, did not recognize him.

"Maddie! It's me! Bobby!"

"Bobby? What the fuck happened to you?"

"Shh! Where's Mr. Jenkins?"

"He's out sick, Isn't that funny? A pharmacist who's sick? He asked me to open up today so now we can have the whole fucking place to ourselves! Isn't that cool? But what the fuck happened to you, man?"

It was almost three, and there wouldn't be that many customers at that time as he pulled her away.

"I erased myself, Maddie. Remember those pencils? And you wouldn't believe me! Well, I guess they only work on me, 'cause now I'm fucking white! And I hate it, Maddie! I hate how people treat me. I mean, I like it too, but I hate it. Shit!

It's all so mixed up! How if you're black, you're treated one way and then when you're white you're treated another way. I just wanted things to be easier. Now, people in my own neighborhood call me a whitey and the white kids at school now become my friends?! What the fuck is wrong with this world, Maddie?"

Maddie flipped the store's OPEN sign to CLOSED.

"Come on, Bobby. Let's go to the locker room."

"You gotta help me, Maddie. Maybe there's like a cream or like an antidote that I can take, so that I can go back to my original color. Please help me, Maddie."

She handed him a small plastic bottle of Evian water.

"Drink this and calm down, ok? I'm gonna go to the soap section to see if I can find something to wash that stuff off. Don't worry Bobby, we'll get you back. Why did you do this to yourself?"

Bobby welcomed the water and Maddie's soothing words, allowing them both to steady him. "Because I see it, Maddie. I mean, how we're treated, and I got sick of it. How the cops harass me, and how the rest of the world treats me like crap because I'm black. And that's when I decided to change it all. To make it easier for me. I felt free, Maddie… free…but now, now, I don't want it. I mean it's cool and shit when you're first in line and nobody bothers you and people make you feel special, like you're above everyone else… because you're white. But it's not so cool when other people call you names because you're not white. Ah, it's all fucked up!"

Maddie carefully listened as she reflectively inhaled her cigarette.

"You're right about that, man, this is really fucked up!"

Maddie stomped out the cigarette. "But we are who we are, Bobby! We can't change that! We gotta respect that! We gotta love ourselves, no matter what!" She lit another cigarette. "Listen, I'm gonna get some stuff from Aisle 2 and I'll be right back! Man, it's a good fucking thing that Mr. Jenkins called in sick."

Bobby sipped the water again wondering how his Titi would react, how she wouldn't even recognize him, like Maddie. He worried that it would hurt her about how he rejected himself and her, and Maddie, for what he truly was.

Maddie raced back into the locker room, her arms filled with at least ten different jars and bottles of body creams and lotions. "Come over here, bro, maybe one of these will work."

As Maddie furiously tried to remove his new skin, Bobby realized that none of it would work. For some reason he knew that he would remain like that forever.

After some time, Maddie decided to close the store sooner than later so that Bobby could go home.

"I'll just let Mr. Jenkins know that I had to close early 'cause you got sick and that I couldn't manage it alone. Maybe you can try those pencils again, Bobby, see if maybe they can bring you back."

Knowing that it would never work, he promised her that he would try.

They rode the uptown train together.

He remembered that his Titi would still be up at that hour and how he would have to explain his new color and why he wanted to change it.

"Listen, Bobby, maybe you should pray, you know, pray to God tonight, see if He can help you with this and don't worry, you'll be yourself soon, I promise."

Maddie kissed him goodbye as she got off at her stop and he continued uptown. She waved at him from the platform as the train passed, blowing him much needed kisses. Bobby felt a chill gurgle up to his throat, wanting to throw up, as he waved back wondering if he would ever see Maddie again.

***

A sleepy Titi Carmen was already in front of the TV half watching the last of the PIX News on Channel 11 as Bobby closed the door behind him.

"Hijo? You're early. I'll heat up some food for you."

Bobby loved his Titi Carmen. She was his only family. Titi Carmen had married once but divorced soon after learning of her husband's infidelity with her best friend. She was alone and childless, but they found in each other a family. He appreciated that.

Bobby slipped into the kitchen wishing that he had a paper bag over his head and his entire body.

"That's okay, Titi. I can do it."

"No, hijo, you work so hard. I'll do it…and…"

Bobby tried to shield himself from her, but it was too late.

"Ai, Dios mio! What is this?"

She pulled him back inside the living room.

"We have to call 911 or go to Emergency…pero, que te paso, hijo? Are you in pain?"

"No, Titi, please it's nothing, really…I'm not in pain."

"Pero, what is this? Was it something en esa pharmacia hijo? Dios! Diosito mío! ¡Pobre hijo!"

Gently he maneuvered her to the couch, shushing her with each step. "No, Titi, it was me, it was me! Please, Titi, please sit down and I'll tell you, okay? Just sit."

And Bobby explained about the box of pencils that he found in the store and how no one seemed to know where they came from and how he wrote his mother's name on his palm and that when he tried to erase it how the unusual eraser not only erased his name but also the color of his true skin and how when he tried it on Maddie, and how it didn't work on her, and how it was almost as if they were made for him to use and only him.

"Don't worry, Titi, me, and Maddie, we're gonna keep trying to find something at the store that can make it go back to how it was, to who I was. I'm sure we'll find something, I promise, Titi."

"Ai, it's all my fault, hijo. It's all my fault! Where are they, Bobby. Los lapis?"

She raced towards his room anxiously pulling at her short, wiry hair.

"We must burn them, hijo, that's the only way that we can fix this mess. Ai, Dios!"

Bobby retrieved his backpack from the floor.

"Titi, I don't understand. I have them here."

His aunt leapt towards the bag as if it were prey.

"Come on, let's go in the kitchen and burn them before they do any more harm!"

"Titi, I don't understand. What are you talking about? Do you know something that I don't?"

"Where are those matches? We must burn them before…"

"Before what? Wait! Please before we do anything, you

have to tell me Titi, about these pencils and about me. Please!"

His aunt sat on one of the metal kitchen chairs as she spoke dejectedly.

"Los reconozco…los reconozco, hijo. They belonged to your mother…"

Bobby's gasp was barely audible as it floated its way through the cramped kitchen.

"Somehow, they have reached you from where she is. Alicia, your mother, que Dios la bendiga, was very unhappy when she first arrived from Cuba. She was the oldest, so she came here, alone, promising to make enough money to send for us, but that day never came, hijo."

Bobby sat opposite her as a tear dropped to her bare knees, creating an incandescent droplet of water upon her smooth black skin.

"But your mother soon learned about this country's racismo, something that she had never experienced in Santiago where everyone is like us, like her, like me and you, negro como nosotros, as black as the depths of the ocean."

Bobby, never having seen his mother, wept for her suffering and what she had to endure.

"Even after she met your father, que en paz descanse, and after your birth, she thought that perhaps one day that ugly hate and anger that she found in this country would go away, pero, no, hijo. Your father's family, unos blancos de Havana, also would not accept her because of her color. So, one day she met a man who promised to change all of that. Un brujo, hijo, de'l Bronx, and he gave her this box to erase her skin color so that she could be accepted in a country that would not accept her and be loved by your father's family. She did as he instructed and each night, after work, she would erase herself, little by little, a shade lighter and lighter, con cada raspadura…. your father, who knew nothing about the pencils, thought it was some sort of skin disease and took her to the doctors, but they could not find anything wrong with her. Until one day, after using all of the pencils' erasers, she changed herself into a white woman, blanca como una paloma. When your father saw her, he was so upset and so frightened that he left! 'I loved you the way you were, Alicia, you were beautiful just as you were!' Your father never came back that day and your mother was heartbroken. The following morning, so early that not even the sun was fully awake, she went back to that brujo and pleaded with him to help her as she felt that without your father there was nothing to live for. The brujo gave her another box. 'These will mend your broken heart.' Your mother scrubbed her skin with those new borradores but soon discovered that they were making her invisible! Desapareció por completo! Until all that was left in the bedroom was this box."

His aunt rose and enveloped him with an ample embrace.

"Your father, who adored your mother, had every intention of returning home, he just wanted to blow off some steam, hijo. Black, white, purple or green, he loved your mother no matter what. But when he returned, she was gone. He searched and searched for her, and even called the police and hired private detectives, never believing that it was those pencils that caused her disappearance. She was gone."

Carmen released Bobby and returned to the chair.

"Days and months went by, hijo, and your father sent for me to come to care for you. Your father did his best to find her, Bobby, until his death from a broken heart when you were only two years old. All the while he kept that box, the only thing that remained of his beautiful esposa and my dear sister. How it got to you inside that store, hijo, is a mystery."

"But how did you know about the pencils, Titi?"

"Right after your father's passing, I found that box in the apartment and I knew it for what it was! Brujeria! So, I found that brujo and he confessed it all to me. I left the box with him hoping never to see him or that box ever again!" Bobby's aunt remained seated, exhausted by the truth.

"She heard me, Titi. My mother sensed how unhappy I was. But now look at me! Either way I can't win, Titi!"

"But you are winning, hijo! You have accomplished so much in this miserable world, on your own, despite everything. Your mother, your father would be so proud. Maybe she did send you that box. Maybe she heard your grief from heaven, and maybe she is using that box to test you, to make sure that you do not disappear like she did so that you can continue in this life. Please don't leave me!"

His aunt was right. He was already completely white, and the next step would be irreversible.

"I gotta get upstairs. I'm so tired, Titi. I'll think about what you said, I promise. I'll think about everything."

"Descansa, hijo. We'll speak more tomorrow." The woman waited until Bobby returned to his room before she opened the box and turned on the clicking gas stove.

"You have already done too much harm!" She held the pencils over the open flame as a fire caught but then extinguished itself. "Pero que…?" Again, the woman tried to burn them, but the blaze would not even scorch them. Soon a putrid stench from the pencils filled the room, choking the woman.

"Demonios!," she screamed as she tossed the pencils back inside the box and opened the kitchen's window allowing the breeze to revive her.

"Dios, Dios mio, protejalo! Por favor, Hermana, Hermana querida, please help your son make the right decision."

At once a strong gust of wind filled the kitchen as Carmen continued to pray aloud. Her heavy body quivered uncontrollably with each desperate plea.

"Padre nuestro, que estás en el cielo, santificado sea tu nombre…"

Bobby had trouble sleeping as he tried his best to remember the mother that he had never seen. Soon the dream entered his mind as she revealed herself: "Hijo, do not blame me. I did the best for you, for us." Her image filled his heart with dazzling light, neither white nor black but golden, his resplendent mother, who spoke to him in sweet, gentle whispers; an uplifting maternal song.

"Hijo, it is time to be with me." She held out the box. "Toma esto, Bobby…you are close to being where you should be, with me, with your father, here in El Paraíso, where there is no unhappiness, no hate, only love, hijo, pure and simple."

She shimmered as if moonbeams lived inside her. "Toma esto…"

He began to erase himself completely of color, any color, feeling the burden lifting itself from his tired spirit, as he drew closer and closer to his mother.

"Just a few more strokes, hijo."

And Bobby continued in the dream as he uncovered the inner shards of sacred light that live beneath the shell, beneath the mask of flesh, and bone, and blood and hue.

"Ven ahora hijo… now there will be no more tears…"

And the reunited mother and child walked together along the celestial path, as his father joined them, moving closer and closer to their home as one.

The following day Titi Carmen had already prepared a splendid breakfast of huevos frito con maduros for Bobby, his favorite, knowing that he would be ravenous.

"Hijo! Despierta! It's getting late. Let's eat together before I go to work. Hijo!"

Titi Carmen turned the stove's knob to "low" as she placed two slices of whole wheat bread in the toaster.

"Hijo, I must leave soon. I wanted us to talk before I go. Pobre nene, he must be exhausted." The woman paused before the kitchen window to open it, noticing how striking the sun was that morning, much shinier and yellower than she had ever seen it before in her life.

"Pero que cosa tan rara…" Instinctively she ran to his room.

"Bobby! Bobby!" Cautiously she opened the door. "Bobby?"

And in the middle of his bed, she found the box, emptied of its contents, the room, vacant of Bobby.

"Bobby!" The woman wept, pained by the loss, as the smell of burning toast filled the extraordinarily luminous room.

THE MANICURIST

Inez had been in the nail salon since early that morning when her boss, Su-Jin, called her to remind her about the exhaust fan.

"Don't forget to turn it on, Inez," her boss explained. "The upstairs neighbors have been complaining to the landlord about the smell."

"Yes, Su-Jin. I won't forget."

Inez was all alone today, Tuesday, one of the slowest days of the week in the shop; only two customers since this morning. The same two who would always come in for repairs on their fake, acrylic nails.

It was the middle of May; still too cool to think about summer although Inez knew that soon they would need to put in an air conditioner. Inez sympathized with the building's neighbors who bitterly complained about the toxins and fumes released by the ground floor salon's hundreds of tiny bottles of nail polish and pervasive acetone.

Inez had already grown used to the pungent odors ever since she was a child in Perquín, El Salvador, where she was born, when she would often help her mother with the manicures for the Americans in the fancy hotels nearby.

The smell from the polish removers and the multitude of bottled nail polish lived inside her pores, becoming a part of her now, a part of her basic scent.

Inez had been working at the shop with Su-Jin, the owner,

and two others for a few years now. The part-time job, done after she had completed her day at school and homework, helped with Nilda's, her mother's friend whom she lived with, bills and such.

But Nilda would always make sure that Inez would first pay attention to her studies before she went to work for Su-Jin.

"First you go to school, Inez and then you work. Without an education in this country, mi'já, you will be lost."

But all of that love and encouragement from Nilda came to an abrupt end after her recent and untimely death from breast cancer. Inez left school to work full-time with Su-Jin, barely able to pay Nilda's rent and all of the other costs of being on her own. In time, Inez had no other choice than to vacate the one bedroom apartment.

Lourdes, one of the other girls in the shop, offered her a bedroom in her mother's three-bedroom in Washington Heights. The deal was a good one for Inez where she would be able to cover all of her expenses and still be able to save a little for her return trip home whenever that would happen.

Inez rose to turn on the tiny fans that sat on each of the little manicuring tables in the shop. She missed Nilda. She missed her mother and her family who seldom wrote for fear of revealing their daughter's location to the American nuns and priests who lived in their village.

Inez recalled the time when the American ministry first arrived in their shiny, new van, accompanied by the military police, which was filled to the brim with much needed medical supplies and school books as well as hundreds of copies of the Bible.

The missionaries were both welcomed and feared by Inez's father, Francisco de la Paz, including Christina, her mother and her uncle, Rafael, and the others in los campos, who cut the sugar cane and cared for the land.

When she wasn't cutting cane in the fields Christina made extra income on the weekends when she would offer her grooming services to the wealthy American tourists.

"When you are a little older Inez, you can work by my side. Until then, mira y aprende," her mother instructed. "One day you will be able to give these *gringas* the best manicure that they have ever had in their lives."

Inez obeyed her mother as she patiently watched her mother transform the pale, dry, nail bitten American hands into beautifully soft, vibrant works of art. For only the cost of one American dollar, Christina worked tirelessly on each hand until all ten nails were meticulously filed and polished. All the customers marveled at her mother's abilities as they reluctantly offered her their wrinkled dollar, never addressing her mother directly or looking her in the eyes.

"You have certainly earned your money!" all of the white women exclaimed. "My nails look divine!"

In time, her mother would allow Inez to assist with the manicures.

"There is something very special about you, Inez. I can always feel it when I hold your hand."

Indeed, Christina noticed something different about her daughter just by the way that Inez would hold her hand when they walked to la marqueta. "You possess something here, hija, deep inside, that everyone will notice."

Christina's mother, Altagracia, a well-known curandera,

known to all as "La India," because of her indigenous features, would soothe people's hurts and pains and aches just with a touch of her hand. Christina knew that Inez had inherited not only her grandmother's physical characteristics, but also this most profound gift.

"You have your Abuela's talent for healing, hija. And it is a very special one."

But Christina also knew that her mother was a clairvoyant who could easily foretell future tragedies or joyous events.

This worried Christina.

Their village, their country, their people had changed considerably since her mother's passing, leaving them all at the mercy of an unpredictable future.

"Be careful, hija. Not everyone is prepared for someone like you."

Inez did not completely understand what her mother told her but was happy enough to be able to perform her first manicure after watching for many months.

"Your mama is making my nails so beautiful, little girl."

The gringa patted Inez's tiny hand as she gave her one of the little cakes of perfumed soaps that the woman had stolen from the hotel.

"One day you can do my nails too, little girl, and make money for your mommy. Wouldn't that be nice?"

Inez passed one of the nail clippers to her mother as she continued to hold the woman's left hand.

Christina worked hard to remove the nicotine stains embedded around the woman's nails' beds while trying not to breathe in the strong whiskey smell from the woman's inebriated breath.

"You will be in a car accident, Señora," Inez said without meaning to say it aloud. "Be careful."

Inez whispered the prophecy not even aware that she was speaking.

"Inez, que te pasa?"

Inez continued to hold the gringa's hand, tighter in her grip.

"I see the car, it's upside down, Mama!"

The woman let go of the child's hand.

"What is this shit? Some sort of joke?" she blurted out drunkenly. "Is this some sort of game?"

The woman raced around the hotel's lobby, her dripping fingertips shaking with exaggerated alarm.

"Manager! Manager! These natives are crazy! Help me! Help me! Manager!"

Christina gathered her tools and paints and grabbed Inez's hand as they ran towards the hotel's exit.

"Vente, hija!"

They raced out into the street as they continued to hear the woman's boozy cries. Inez knew that she had done something terribly wrong.

"Mamá, Mamá! Que paso?"

In that moment Christina realized that indeed her daughter had also inherited her mother's blessing of sight. And this deeply concerned her.

When they finally arrived home, Christina nervously prepared that evening's dinner as Inez sat near her playing with the rag doll that one of the missionary teachers had awarded for her near perfect homework done in English.

"Hija, you must promise me never to say to anyone what

you see. Do you understand?"

Inez played with the doll and heard her mother's wishes, but did not really understand.

"I can see it, Mama, what will happen to them, when I hold their hands. I'm sorry. I promise. I won't tell."

Christina sighed deeply as she prepared the red and green peppers for the pollo guisado con batatas.

"Si, hija, it's not your fault. Take this to your Papi and uncle in the fields. Hurry before it gets cold."

The little girl carefully laid her doll on the shack's dark, wood floor. Christina watched as Inez carried the flamboyera, nearly as tall as she, to the men. Christina now knew that her daughter would never be able to control the visions that would come to her so easily and how now it was of utmost importance that she does her best to protect her.

***

Inez sat at her workstation waiting for customers.

Inez never told Su-Jin and the others as to why her mother sent her to America to live with Nilda.

In time, Inez's clientele had grown to a steady one and one that would tip generously amazed by Inez's talents. All Inez knew was that Su-Jin was happy with the burgeoning and well-paying customers. She did not need to know anything else.

Inez opened the shop's door wider.

It was a clear sky; blue color dotted with bunches of white clouds that looked like the cotton balls stuffed in the vitamin jars that she would purchase at the Rite Aid down the block.

The sun and sky and the coming warm breezes always made her think of home and when, if ever, she would return.

"Hola, mami. I just want the regular."

Before Inez could even address Doña Flora, one of the Tuesday regulars, she had already taken a seat at Inez's station.

"Tu eres la única, mi'ja, la única, who I would permit to touch my hands, sabes?"

Inez felt light-headed as she approached her table.

She knew that she had eaten a big breakfast earlier so she couldn't understand what it was that was now making her so unsteady.

"Que te pasa, hija? You look a little pale."

"Nada, nada, Doña. I guess I just need some fresh air."

Doña Flora, not really interested in Inez's health, lifted her right hand as she admired it.

"Be careful, hija? Estás embarazada?" she laughed, displaying a gold tooth in her back molar. "Mira, I want you to work really hard on these pobre nails of mine. Look how brittle they have become!"

Despite Doña Flora's conceit Inez really liked her and admired how hard a worker she was; a seamstress at one the factories in the garment district where pricking sewing machine needles made factory workers' fingertips bleed and cracked.

Inez gently dipped the woman's hand into a small bowl filled with a soapy liquid that would soften the nail bed making it easier to trim and remove the excess flesh.

"Now, let's see, Doña. What have we got here?"

Inez felt lightheaded again, recalling how this would happen many times before with other customers in the shop and when she was a child with her mother in Perquín.

And she remembered her promise.

A promise made to her mother, long ago, of never revealing her secret to anyone.

"Perhaps we should leave this for another day, Doña. I'm not feeling too well…"

"No, hija, you must do them today," Doña Flora demanded as her double-chins jiggled in place. "I have dinner at my nuera's and I must look my best! What will she say behind my back when she sees these disgusting nails? No, hija, I insist that you do them today. I will pay you double my tip!"

Inez stared down at the woman's hands not wanting to touch them again. Ever again.

"Please Inez, you're the only one who can do it."

Inez relented as she lifted her file and began with the work.

She would keep her promise to her mother and find a way to tell Doña Flora of her future without telling the secret like how she did before with the other customers whose hands spoke so clearly to her of their fate.

"That's a good girl, hija," assured Doña Flora. "The fan will help you feel better. Maybe you're coming down with a cold. You just keep working and soon you will feel better."

But with each nail Inez did not feel better, seeing the vision clearer and clearer in her head, right in front of her opened eyes, of the injured Doña Flora, in her flowered dress, soaked in blood and the red spot growing larger and larger with each nail, blinding her with its intensity.

"No!"

Inez threw down the hand and turned in her chair away

from the woman.

"Pero qué cosa?"

"Perdóname, Doña, but I just don't think…"

Doña Flora was insistent. She grabbed a hold of Inez's arm turning her violently towards her.

"No, hija, you do not understand. Please finish your work or I will tell your boss, esa China, that you are lazy…"

Inez could tell that Doña Flora really didn't mean to be so cruel.

"Please hija, " pleaded Dona Flora. "I really need this done today. Por favor."

Inez recalled that Doña Flora had once told her how difficult it was seeing her only son, Peter, since he got married.

"Tomorrow will be the first night that I have been invited to their home. I want to look my best for Peter, for his wife. I want only the best for them. Por favor, Inez."

Inez continued with the work. She expertly filed and buffed each nail and then applied the polish, closing her eyes with every stroke to hide the terrifying vision from her view. Then, upon completion, Inez made the sign of the cross upon each of Doña Flora's nails. She had done this before with her other customers who were about to experience an unavoidable tragedy; a sign of the cross on each filed, buffed and polished nail; a talisman for protection.

With each up and down and horizontal stroke, Inez recited a silent prayer, asking God to protect Doña Flora and all of the others; keeping them safe without ever breaking her promise to her mother.

And then she saw it: another vision.

Doña Flora would survive the horrific car crash.

She would be fine.

The prayers always worked.

"They're beautiful, hija! Gracias! Gracias!"

Not even Doña Flora noticed what Inez had done with each nail as she prayed for Doña Flora's safety.

"Te lo debo, hija."

Doña Flora gave her more than double her usual tip, just as she had promised, as she exited the salon while happily singing a sad bolero.

Inez closed the door and went to the tiny stereo that Su-Jin kept in the supply room hoping that the lively salsa music would lift her spirits. As she fiddled with the radio's dial Inez wondered if she should have done more for Doña Flora and the others.

"No, the prayers have always been more than enough. It's best that I keep quiet, like Mama told me to, or they will find me," she murmured as she continued to search for a clear reception.

The music filled the small shop as Inez re-filled the soap dish recalling her mother's words.

"It's as if she is speaking directly to God," she explained to her husband Francisco. "We must do something."

They decided, despite their better judgment, to speak to one of the Catholic missionaries in their village about Inez's psychic abilities.

"*Signoura,*" mispronounced the American nun. "This is a serious matter and one that we must take to Father Everett."

Inez noticed the nun's green teeth and wondered if she had eaten too many unripe panapen.

"Come with me immediately!"

Father Everett was nearly six foot tall and obese. He always wore his black suit and the white starched collar despite the oppressive heat that would overtake the villagers especially just before the summer rains came. Inez had seen him before in the village's school for the boys where she would sneak off to when her own class, with the girls, was in recess.

Father Everett spoke calmly but sternly to the class with a sinister tone that would always frighten Inez.

"No, no, Enrique, how many times must I repeat myself to you? Are you an idiot?"

Inez always took note of how the young boys, some barefoot, some not, always sat so still in their seats as if each of them had rods of steel in their spines rather than flesh and bone.

"Come to the head of the class, Enrique."

Inez recognized the boy as the son of Ismael, their neighbor, a farmer who harvested and sold coffee beans. Enrique had been having trouble memorizing the daily English vocabulary lessons and began to weep knowing what was in store for him.

"No crying, Enrique. You know how this works."

Inez was bewildered at how the man in black who was obviously so upset could speak so calmly.

It petrified her.

"Pull them down, Enrique."

The boy said nothing, allowing the tears to flow fiercely down his tiny red cheeks as he undid his trousers and stood there before the class. "And now the underpants, my son."

Inez wanted to scream for help or run into the classroom and stop the assault, but she couldn't. She just couldn't.

The priest stood close to Enrique as he tapped, tapped, tapped a long, flat wooden ruler, that was almost as tall as Enrique, inside his fat palm.

"This hurts me more than you, my son."

Father Everett lifted the ruler up and behind his shoulders, the way Papi would do with the machete to cut the tall weeds in their fields.

"Bend over, Enrique."

Inez tightly closed her eyes as she heard each whack against the boy's flesh, struggling to bury the memory of Enrique's cries away in her head. But it quickly resurfaced as soon as the nun mentioned Father Everett's name.

"Of course, Hermana," said Inez's mother. "We will speak with Padre Everett."

Christina took Inez's hand as they followed behind the flustered nun who rapidly made the sign of the cross over and over again across her flattened breasts.

"Such things are works of the devil, *signoura*! We must act promptly and do all we can to save this poor innocent little girl." Inez pulled at her mother's hand wanting to tell her about Enrique.

"Mama, please I don't want to go."

Christina paused and looked into her daughter's brown face now nearly white from fear.

She really didn't like these people; these foreigners who would insist that the villagers speak their language before they would even try to learn and speak Spanish. She didn't like how they would call them names, as if they were salvajes. And she didn't like how they would force them to attend Sunday mass when it was the only day that they could rest from the work in the fields and her endless trips to the hotels. She didn't appreciate how they would force them to learn the words to their prayers in English and recite them to wooden images when all her life all she would have to do was address the sky, or the trees or their beautiful river and know that God was listening.

She did not like them, not at all, but they brought with them much needed medical supplies and books for their children that they could not afford on their own. She did not like them, she did not trust them, but her daughter was getting bigger each day and learning from their school.

She recalled how her mother suffered and how it was both a blessing and a curse to be a prophet.

"But we must go, Inez. It's for your own good. I want you to be happy."

She was very happy. Couldn't her mother see that?

"Come on. If he doesn't help us, I promise you that I will never take you to them again."

Inez was confused. Should she tell her mother about what the priest did to Enrique and get scolded for sneaking away to the boys' school and risk getting punished?

Inez decided to suffer the consequences rather than meeting with the priest.

"Mama, please, I have to tell you something…"

But it was too late as her mother and the jittery nun found the priest standing near the boys' school.

"We have a problem, Father…a serious one. Satan has possessed this poor, innocent child. We must act now to rescue her from his evil doings."

The nun made the sign of the cross again as Inez felt her

mother's hand tightening its grasp.

"Por favor, Padre, Inez es mi hija…necesito ayuda…por favor…"

The priest squatted down to Inez as he looked directly into her eyes causing Inez's heart to race as the tiny hairs on her brow bristled from his foul fish breath.

"Now, now, there's nothing to be afraid of, child."

He took Inez by the hand as he led her to the small church nearby.

"Come with me into the house of God, dear child, and tell me what it is that is troubling you."

Inez glanced again at her mother silently pleading for her help.

"Vete, hija. El cura will help you."

Father Everett continued to hold her hand as Inez felt the squishy wetness from his palm seeping into hers.

"Speak to me, child, tell me what you feel."

Inez watched as her mother sat in one of the pews near the altar of the crucified martyr.

"Padre…Father…I *see*…"

Father Everett shifted uncomfortably in his stiff uniform. Inez noticed large round wet black stains underneath his arms and his increasing yellowing collar.

"See? What do you see, child?"

Even when she wasn't manicuring someone's hands, even if she just held their hands, the way that Father Everett now held hers, she could see what would happen to them.

"I see you Father…the villagers are angry…they are around you Father screaming loudly…they do not want you here no more, Padre…"

Father Everett removed his hand from Inez's grasp.

"What else do you see, child?"

The vision disappeared as soon as he let go.

"Nada, Padre…only when I hold your hand, Padre…"

Father Everett stood up from the bench as he looked down at Inez.

"That's very good, child. You can go back to your Mama."

Inez was elated. Not only did she not have to pull down her panties and get a beating, but she didn't even have to tell her mother about Enrique and risk getting one.

"Sister, may I speak to you in private?"

The uneasy nun flocked to his side, the ends of her black habit slapping in the wind like an intoxicated crow.

Christina took Inez by the hand and led her out of the church.

"What did you say to the Padre, Inez? What did he say to you?"

But before Inez could answer, the nun hurried back to them.

"Father Everett thinks that it might be best that we speak to the authorities about Inez."

Christina instinctively shielded her daughter away from the people of God.

"I don't understand, Hermanita. We wish only for your help."

Christina's heart sank to the bottom of her feet. She had done something wrong. She knew that speaking to the authorities meant only one thing.

"Father Everett thinks that perhaps little Inez might be able to help them with the rebels."

The nun patted the top of Inez's head soaking it with her clammy hand.

"You see those heathens, the ones in the mountains? They have been causing a lot of mischief with the authorities and perhaps little Inez here might be able to help sniff them out."

The nun breathed in through her nose imitating the sound of a hungry dog.

"Intiendos?"

Inez tried not to laugh at the nun's ignorance.

"If you do not agree to help us, *signoura*, we will have no other choice than to seek custody of Inez as a ward of the state."

Christina's heart shattered.

She wanted to kick herself for being so stupid.

Her brother, Rafael, would often speak to them, late at night, in whispers, while Inez slept, of his solidarity with the Freedom Fighters who hid in the mountains.

"Hermana, please you must understand, they are our people. We must do all we can to help them. We must protect our country."

Christina and Francisco knew that he was right as they pledged to aid the revolutionists, with assistance from a priest in San Miguel who was later assassinated in his own church by the military police for his efforts.

But now, as she and Inez waved goodbye to the nun, she knew that she had not only placed the guerreros' lives in danger but also that of her child.

"We will see you early tomorrow morning at the church Christina, and please bring your daughter."

Christina cringed and began to tremble.

As soon as they got home Christina informed Francisco and Rafael about what happened.

"We must act soon, Christina," explained Rafael. "I will leave with Inez tonight."

Christina looked at her daughter trying not to weep.

"Hija, I cannot allow those people in the church to use your talent to hurt us, to hurt me and your papa and Tio and the ones who fight for our freedom. Do you understand? They will never take you away from me!"

Inez nodded but she really didn't understand anything at all. Later her mother returned after using the neighbor's telephone to make a long-distance call to an old friend in Nueva York.

"Apúrate, Inez. We must get ready for your trip with Tio."

Christina packed a tiny valise made from cloth that she had sewn, with Inez's clothes and her doll, and instructed her to go with her uncle to los campos where they would meet his friends.

"You're going to America, hija. Isn't that wonderful?"

But Inez could not understand how something so exciting could make her mother cry.

"I will write to you and Tia Nilda in Nueva York. Que Dios te bendiga."

Inez and her uncle were picked up by his friend, Luis, who owned a dilapidated pickup truck that would take them to their first destination.

"We have a long way to go, sobrina," explained her uncle. "Please get some rest."

With the full moon as their only light, Inez climbed into

the vehicle as she watched the dark figures of her parents blending into the night sky, waving their goodbyes and promising a speedy reunion.

"No te apures, hija. We will be together again soon…te quiero! Te quiero mucho!"

She heard her mother's choking voice in the cold wind until she heard it no more, could see them no more.

"By the time you awake, hija, you will be closer to America."

Inez placed her tilted head onto her Tio's shoulder and soon the dream came.

Inez saw herself holding her treasured doll, waving goodbye to her parents, as she stood alone in the dark road near her home. But soon the moon's light was overcome by a looming shadow over their tiny shack, over her parents, engulfing them with its darkness.

"Mama, Papa!"

Inez looked over the house as their figures were completely covered leaving her alone and lost in the rustic void.

"Mama!"

Rafael roused her gently as she struggled to wake.

"Inez, you were dreaming. Come, it's time for the next part of our journey."

He lifted her out of the truck as they walked towards a group of four young men, all carrying large rifles.

"Compañeros!"

The young men embraced as Rafael introduced them to Inez.

"Inez, you will go with these men, and they will protect

you."

Again Inez began to weep not wanting to let go. She had already seen her uncle's future, as she held his hand in the truck, but dared not utter a word of what was to come.

"No, no, hija, this is for the best. Please trust me, y no llores, Inez. You must go!"

"But, Tio, please…I saw something…I saw you…"

Her Tio kissed Inez's cold cheek warming it with his confidence.

"I know, Inez. I know what will happen. I can see too, just like Mama, just like you. Now it's time for your wonderful journey."

But Inez could not move as one of the men, who looked like Rafael, tall, dark and strong, gently took her hand and led her to the caravan already filled with other people, children, men and women, just like her who would travel to a different world.

"I will take care of you, Inez. What is your muñeca's name? Would you like some dulce de leche?"

Inez accepted the treat from the man. The candy nearly stopped her from crying, but not really.

"No tengas miedo, chiquita," consoled another one of the passengers, a woman. "We will all be safe with our courageous, young caballeros protecting us."

Inez looked out towards Rafael who stood resolute, side to-side with the other soldiers.

"Adios, Inez. I will stay here with the others," he cried. "We will all be together soon. Te lo prometo!"

Inez waved weakly to him as the van drove away, his image disappearing gradually into his merciless destiny.

The driver, an older man, informed the passengers of their journey ahead.

"Once we have reached Mexico we will meet yet another compañero. From there we will reach the border where many of your friends will be there to greet you."

Inez remembered what her mother said about Tia Nilda and wondered if she would be able to recognize someone she had never met.

"Many of you will stay in Texas," he continued. "While others are destined for Nueva York."

Inez immediately felt a little better when she remembered the city that her mother told her about where Tia Nilda lived as she wondered just how close Texas and New York were from each other.

The long ride proved to be one that carried its share of bumps, stops and starts, as Inez rested her head on her doll's body. In time Inez opened her eyes and found herself on the third leg of the long journey to America. While the others disembarked the truck, Inez remained alone.

"Do not worry, hija," the sympathetic driver explained. "I'm sure that your guardian will be here soon."

Inez clutched her doll closer, feeling so alone.

"Inez! Inez de la Paz?"

Inez leaped out of her seat and saw the man wave to her.

"I was sent by Señora Nilda Alvarez. Please come with me!"

The man helped her with her little sack and her doll as they climbed into yet another van with several other passengers.

"First stop, Corpus Christi!"

Everyone applauded at the mention of the words as they

made their way towards the faraway land.

Many hours passed as Inez ate some of the food that the driver supplied.

"It's a long trip, mi'ja. Eat up!"

The food made her sleepy as Inez prayed for another opportunity to dream about her parents.

In time, the heat of the new sun woke her as the driver's words rang out to greet her in the unfamiliar country and her final stop.

"Buena suerte, little one and welcome to America!"

The woman who greeted them was tall and slim and wore a beige suit and a flowered shirt.

"Inez?"

Inez ran towards her, collapsing into the waiting arms of Tia Nilda as the strong woman carried her off to a plane headed towards New York.

The years flew by as Tia Nilda and Inez became close friends using their time together to learn English and read books to each other.

Nilda, a retired teacher from Puerto Rico, was not really her Tia, but someone that her mother had met while Nilda was vacationing in El Salvador.

"I met your mother at one of the hotels and we became friends. I admired her commitment and her devotion to her family and her country. Since then we have corresponded regularly. When she called to tell me about what happened with the priest I thought it best that you were here with me, safe and sound, Inez."

Inez wondered how being with Nilda was safe and sound when all she wanted was to be with her own family. But Inez grew to love Nilda as her second mother and was by her side, holding her hand, to the very end.

"Tia, I can see where you are going and it is a beautiful place. You will not suffer any more."

"Gracias, hija."

After her death, Inez found comfort in knowing that Nilda's spirit would always watch over and guide her.

***

After Doña Flora left the shop Inez went to each of the small nail stations to assemble the grooming instruments.

"Hola, Inez! Are you ready to do me?"

Lourdes burst into the salon obviously skipping her afternoon high school classes in favor of having her acrylic tips done.

"Why aren't you in school?"

Inez lived with Lourdes and her mother near the shop. Lourdes' mother, Mrs. Dominquez, a pleasant woman, who worked during the day and often at night as a cleaning woman. She was determined to see that Lourdes complete her studies and go on to college.

Inez envied Lourdes. Inez would never be able to finish high school now that Tia Nilda was gone. Did she not know how lucky she was?

"I got a big date tonight with Manny."

Lourdes chewed her gum loudly and would often snap it as she spoke; a habit that irritated Inez when Lourdes worked at the shop on the weekends and sometimes after school.

"He said he got something to tell me. Something special.

And I think I know what it is! Oooo!"

Lourdes joyfully spun herself in the chair.

"Inez, I think he's gonna ask me to marry him!"

Inez stopped in her tracks, nearly knocking over the tiny bottles of pink and red polish at her station.

"What? Estas loca?"

"Don't tell, Mami, ok? Don't even tell her that I'm going out tonight. It's a school night. Just tell her that I'm with Sandra over at 168th Street."

Inez did not want to deny her but knew that Manny was no good. No good at all.

"Lourdes, te quiero and you know how much I appreciate all that you and your mother have done for me…but I cannot continue to lie."

Lourdes grabbed Inez's hands.

"Please, querida, I'm sorry to put you in the middle all the time but you gotta do this for me, please!"

As she worked on Lourdes' hands Inez saw a passing vision, a glimpse, but it went by too fast and was too blurry to fully understand it.

"This will be the last time, te lo prometo, Inez. After this, Manny and I will live together so there won't be a reason to lie, entiendes?"

Inez wished to bite her tongue but decided it was better to speak than not.

"Manny is too possessive, Lourdes! He is constantly spying and asking around. His jealousy is dangerous. I do not think that he is the best one for you, Lourdes. I'm sorry."

Lourdes angrily stood up from the chair.

"So, what's the big fucking deal? He's jealous! I like it

when he's jealous anyway. It keeps him on his toes!"

"I don't know, Lourdes. It's good to be a little jealous but it's not good to be so possessive. Cuidado, Lourdes, cuidado."

Lourdes returned to her seat and placed both her hands out to Inez.

"Oh, come on be happy for me, Inez. If you make these hands beautiful, like I know you will, I'll make you my maid of honor, ok?"

Inez couldn't help but be amused by her friend's charm as she held her tiny hands in hers and massaged them.

But in an instant the panic returned and Inez let go of Lourdes' hands.

"What's wrong, Inez? Come on, hurry up! After this, I have to pick up my dress at the dry cleaners and then after that I gotta get my hair straightened and you know how long that takes…what's wrong?"

Without looking into her eyes Inez took Lourdes' hands back into hers.

"There you go, nena. Just file them a little and put on a fresh coat of this one…the purple one."

Soon Inez saw it all. What would happen to her, to Lourdes, her friend, that night, with Manny at the club. And she saw Lourdes in the club waiting for him, as he instructed, standing with other patrons, drinking, laughing, dancing, Lourdes, the curvaceous girl, with cinnamon eyes, in her pretty, sequin honey-colored gown, that fell down to the floor, its woven train fluttering with Lourdes' every dance step, resembling Ochún, the goddess of sweetness and love from her ancestors' country, her rippled hair, long and black, a vivid sheen that cascaded down her sides like a river, flirting with the other cute guys, a harmless flirt, with her favorite drink, Cuba Libre, and she felt free, and young, and happy, winking, and swaying her voluptuous hips to the rhythmic bata drums of the merengue and the bachata from the Dominican band, a veritable bembé that played the sounds of the eternal deities that demanded the worshipful dance and homage to be paid in honor of the indigenous soul, and all of the others, spiritual brothers and sisters, who enjoyed their lives and their time together, and as always, always mindful of her loyalty dance to Manny, undeserved loyalty, as Manny arrived in his car at the club, *Dream Land*, where the people would go to find their dreams and be joyful, away from the hardship of their lives, but this would not be a happy dream, but a nightmare, as Manny went to the car's trunk and retrieved a plastic container as he unscrewed the cap, moving towards the nightclub, throwing splashes of the gasoline around and inside the building, secretively, where no one would see, no one could see him except Inez, here, now, as she held Lourdes' hands, as the vision became clearer and clearer inside her opened eyes, as she saw Lourdes and the others, innocently enjoying their lives, not a care in the world, Lourdes the expectant bride, and she did not even know it yet that she was carrying his child, waiting for her beloved groom, who continued to soak the building, its emergency exits bolted shut by negligent owners, with the dangerous liquid as he lit a match.

Inez closed her eyes shut wanting it all to go away, the vision, wanting it all to disappear and to never happen.

"Ow! Inez! You're hurting me! Let go!"

"Perdóname me, Lourdes," said Inez as she let go of her friend's hands but then abruptly grabbed them again. "Please,

Lourdes, you cannot go tonight! Please do not go! Te lo pido, no vayas!"

"You're hurting me, Inez," protested Lourdes. "What the fuck is wrong with you, girl?

Inez wanted so much to tell her and all of the others, what it was that she saw, about how she saw things before they happened, to warn her about Manny and the fire that he would set at the club, and the patrons there defenseless, and Lourdes, pregnant, unknowing of the baby inside her, she saw it all and she wanted to tell Lourdes and Doña Flora but she couldn't, she promised her mother and even Tia Nilda, her parting last words to her, that she would never tell her secret to anyone or they would come for her and kill her parents and the Freedom Fighters and she would never see them again.

No, she could not tell them, but she could warn her and try to protect her.

"Please Lourdes, listen to me. It's Manny, he's out of control and it's possible for him to do anything to hurt you. Please do not go tonight. Please stay home with me and we can read books and talk about our lives, our dreams. Please."

Lourdes sighed loudly as she returned to her seat. She knew that Inez was lonely and that she wanted to have a normal life, a normal American life, like hers, going to school, meeting boys, dating.

"Listen, Inez. After we get married you, Manny and me, we can all go out to the movies and have fun. And maybe Manny can introduce you to one of his friends so that you can have a boyfriend too, ok? Mira, I have my hair appointment with Martiza at three and you know how she gets when people are late. I'll do my own nails later."

Lourdes had already crossed to the store's exit before Inez could reach her and at least protect her with the sign of the cross on each of her nails.

"Wait, Lourdes! I must finish the manicure or else…" Lourdes reached into her purse.

"Here, mami! Catch!"

She threw a five dollar bill in the air towards Inez.

"Just in case you're worried about your tip. Listen, I gotta run! Wish me luck, nena!"

Lourdes walked out of the salon as Inez raced after her but what could she say without revealing everything and breaking her promise to her mother?

She remembered that Dream Land was near Dyckman, not too far from where they lived.

Inez vowed to meet Manny there to stop him. The plan calmed her as she returned to her station. Inez sincerely believed that there was a way to help others without breaking her promise to her mother as she sat to wait for Su-Jin's call to go home and prepare herself for the rescue.

Lourdes' mother, Mrs. Dominquez, worked long painful hours making it even more convenient for her only child to stay out late with her friends and return home in time, safely in her bed, without her mother suspecting a thing.

Mrs. Dominquez was a hardworking woman whose husband died many years ago when Lourdes was a baby.

Not once, in the time that she stayed with them, did Inez ever see her take a day or a night off.

It was always about work and making enough money to save up for a house of her own in Utuado where one day she would retire and live in peace with Lourdes.

It was already nearly 9pm and Inez had just arrived from the salon. Even for a Tuesday it was a long day.

But Inez knew that the visions were exhausting her as well as her promise not to divulge anything. She knew that Lourdes was already on her way to the club so she gave herself a few minutes to eat something before she would leave to stop Manny. Inez knew that she would return in time without Mrs. Dominquez ever suspecting a thing.

"Hola, I'm home, hijas!"

Inez's heart sank as she greeted the exhausted mother at the door.

"Doña! You're home early!

Mrs. Dominquez, a heavy-set woman, who moved sluggishly, removed her coat and peeled off the white leather sneakers that were tightly wrapped around her swollen feet.

"Ai, hija, there was a big mix-up, and I was sent home. It's just as well. I have been working like a dog for the last months and I could use a little rest. Dónde está Lourdes?"

What could she do now? Inez knew that she had to leave at that very moment to be able to stop Manny.

"Lourdes? Well, I don't know, uh, Doña. May I fix you some coffee?"

The tired woman, still dressed in her one-piece gray uniform, reached for the television's remote.

"No, gracias, mi amor. Un poquito de agua."

Inez walked into the kitchen. She had to leave now.

"Gracias, mi'ja. Y Lourdes?"

Inez knew that time was running out as she saw a flash of her vision, the vision of the crazed lover, retrieving the flammable container from his car's trunk.

"Doña, please. I'm late for my appointment."

The woman was already engaged by the news on the TV of the continued strife in El Salvador.

"Esos pobres. During war, it is always the poor who suffer more. Appointment, hija? Con quien?"

Mrs. Dominquez knew from her daughter that Inez did not have many friends, if any at all. All she did was work, like her, and she respected her for this.

Her own daughter, Lourdes, well, she was already a typical American teenager, a little lazy and very spoiled. But, nonetheless, she did her best for her daughter and with Inez now with them, perhaps she might prove to be a good influence on her high-spirited child.

"I promised Su-Jin that I would go over with her…los… los billes…con los servicios and productos…what does she call it?"

"Inventory, Inez. Inventory"

"Si, Señora. Inventory."

"Pero tan tarde, mi'ja? I don't understand. Esa Su-Jin is a hard-working woman like me but I have never heard of this before. But if she is expecting, you must hurry before it is too late. I do not want you wandering the streets after 11pm!"

Inez turned to leave realizing that in fact it might already be too late.

"Y Lourdes, hija? Where is she?"

Inez sighed loudly as she anxiously flung her shoulder bag around her body.

"Doña, I don't know…she was not here when I arrived from the salon."

Mrs. Dominquez lifted herself, with some difficulty, from the couch leaving behind a deep impression on the cushion that had absorbed her weariness.

"Not here? No lo creo. She is always here when you arrive."

The woman entered the kitchen and re-entered the living room holding a pot of white rice.

"You see, Lourdes always cooks the rice for us. She was here. But now she is not."

Mrs. Dominquez menacingly approached Inez with the pot of cold rice.

"Do you know where she is?"

Inez never lied to Mrs. Dominquez and now it seemed as if she needed to make up several.

"Doña, please I cannot tell you. I cannot say…"

Mrs. Dominquez ran into the kitchen and slammed down the pot on top of the small four-burner stove.

"I see it in your eyes, Inez. What is it? Tell me? Is Lourdes in trouble? Where is she? Please tell me."

Mrs. Dominquez took Inez in her arms, locking her securely between herself and her demands for an explanation.

"Dime!"

"Doña, I cannot say. Por favor…I promised Mami."

Mrs. Dominquez released her as she raced towards the cordless phone near the television.

"Your mother? What is she to do with Lourdes? I don't understand. I'm calling the police."

Inez was in trouble. The police, like Father Everett, were on the side of those who tried to hunt her down and hurt her and her family, and her uncle's friends who lived secretly in the mountains. Inez knelt before the woman.

"No! Por favor, Doña. I will tell you!"

Mrs. Dominquez put down the receiver and stared down at the young girl.

"Lourdes, she is with Manny...I'm sorry...I tried to talk her out of going but she insisted...she said that they would be married...that they were to meet at the Dream Land Club and start their future together...and now that you know, I must go..."

Inez hurried towards the door hoping that she could stop Manny from committing the murders.

"Where are you going? You will stay here. I am very disappointed in you, Inez."

Mrs. Dominquez laced back on her work shoes.

"You said that you would never lie to me, Inez, and now you have hidden the truth about Lourdes. Ademas, you knew that she was up to no good con ese sangano, Manny, and yet you do nothing. ¡Qué vergüenza!"

"No! Doña, you don't understand. I must go and stop Manny!"

That was it. Inez had broken her promise. In that moment Inez felt cursed; cursed to be the one to see things that would happen; banished from her home and country because of it. And now cursed to be called a liar.

"Stop Manny? What are you talking about, Inez? Stop him from what?"

Inez would say no more as she saw him again. Manny lighting the match outside Dream Land while Lourdes, now inside the club, was busy dancing and dreaming of a married life that would never be. It was too late.

Inez was too late.

"Nothing, Doña. Nothing."

Mrs. Dominquez unlocked the front door.

"When I return with Lourdes not only will she be punished but I will have to punish you as well, Inez, for your mentiras. Do you understand?"

"Si, Doña."

Inez went into the living room as she began to weep, clearly seeing the man starting the flames that would engulf Lourdes and the others trapped and burning them alive in the intentionally sealed club that would become their crypt.

She knew that they would all perish, and it would be her fault that she could not stop the madman and prevent the deaths. She could no longer continue to uphold her vow to her mother and would either have to break it or else find refuge elsewhere. In time, Inez heard the fire trucks' sirens wailing down the wide avenues of Broadway up and across toward Dyckman. It was indeed too late.

Inez wept into her palms seeing it all unfold in her visions, and how Manny, realizing what he had done, returned to his car and found his small gun inside the glove compartment. Manny would now find remorse in the bullet that he would fire into his brain, joining the other dead bodies that the firemen would find on the crowded dance floor.

***

In the following days Su-Jin accompanied Inez to Lourdes' burial at St. Raymond's cemetery in the Bronx.

"She was a good girl. What a shame."

Inez held onto Su-Jin's hands as the pallbearers carried Lourdes' long, silver and green steel coffin towards her final home.

Mrs. Dominquez threw dirt and wilted red roses on the closed coffin. Inez was broken, knowing that she had a chance to stop Manny and perhaps even save Lourdes and the others. But to tell them what she saw, to tell them of her ability to see, would have meant death to her own family.

Mrs. Dominquez stood in front of Inez - her body slumped over with grief.

"I want you gone, Inez," she groaned. "Do not come back home. I don't ever want to see you again. I will report you to La Migra! Tu me entiendes?"

Su-Jin pulled Inez closer to her.

"Mrs. Dominquez, I know that you are upset but to do such a thing to Inez would be unforgivable. If you report Inez, that would not bring back sweet Lourdes."

Inez was grateful for Su-Jin's words. She knew that Su-Jin, an immigrant from South Korea, was placing herself and all that she worked for, in jeopardy.

"You know as I do, Mrs. Dominquez, that we are all in this together."

Inez recently learned that Su-Jin received her permanent visa and was already on her way to becoming an American citizen.

Mrs. Dominquez paid no attention to Su-Jin's protests as she faced Inez, nearly spitting into her face as she spoke.

"You knew everything, Inez. You knew about what Lourdes was up to con ese asesino! Why didn't you stop her?"

Inez tried to speak to remind Mrs. Dominquez of her

love for Lourdes and how she did try.

"You could have stopped her! You could have stopped her. You are dead to me!"

Sin-Jin moved Inez from the daughter-less woman as the others pulled Mrs. Dominquez away from the encounter.

"Lourdes, Lourdes," howled the fallen women. "Hija! Querida, hija! Mi'ja!"

The cemetery's patrons shuffled away from the mourning as they comforted the woman with their consolations and supplications. The priest closed his Bible. The gravediggers arrived - their boots caked with the stiff mud of the burial. They lowered the coffin into the deep hole.

"Lourdes! Hija, mia!"

Mrs. Dominquez's shrieks resonated as she departed the hallowed field.

"Inez! I will never forget this! I will never forgive you! Te lo juro! Te lo juro!"

"Come on, Inez," whispered Su-Jin. "You come to live with me."

Su-Jin knew that she might get into trouble with her visa and everything that she worked for, gone, poof! Just like that!

How it would all disappear if the INS learned of the young girl's illegal status in the country from Mrs. Dominquez. But she was once in those same shoes when she arrived here and there were those who sacrificed their safety for her, as she would do now for Inez.

"No, Su-Jin. Mrs. Dominquez is right. I could have stopped it. I could have done something."

Su-Jin pulled her away from the coffin as the gravediggers continued with their work, rocking the casket and its content, side to side, lowering it and returning Lourdes back to the earth.

"Come on, Inez. Let's get some coffee. You're just tired. You did nothing. Do not blame yourself."

"No! You don't understand!"

Inez broke free from Su-Jin. She tried to leap into the tomb with Lourdes.

"I'm sorry, Lourdes!"

The gravediggers stopped shoveling as they paused to stare blankly at the weeping girl. Su-Jin pulled her away gently, firmly, determined to leave the anguish behind them.

***

"You're upset, Inez. You don't know what you're saying. Come on, come stay with me. I have plenty of room. It's just me and my cat, Sheba. You know Sheba? She's a little bitch sometimes but she's very sweet."

Inez almost laughed. She never heard Su-Jin curse even with the fussiest customers.

"That's it. Now, we'll go get some coffee and talk about it. How does that sound? Does that sound ok?"

Inez walked with her, hand in hand, away from the dead, recalling the vision about Manny and Lourdes and the others as another vision appeared about Su-Jin. Su-Jin, a woman now nearly in her late forties, who always worked very hard for what she had achieved and now the rewards would finally arrive, as Inez saw her in a wedding gown, holding violets in a church, marching down the aisle towards a man, who wore a dark blue suit, standing before the altar, mature and serene, just as lovely as Su-Jin, as they held hands and made their cherished vows together.

"I see things, Su-Jin."

Su-Jin had always known that there was something special about Inez. Even the customers sensed it. It was more than the perfect manicure. Much more than that.

And she felt it now, as Inez held her hand, feeling her energy running through her and into her soul, knowing that the young girl was blessed with some kind of magic, like the special ones in Seoul, who could tell you of the omens, good ones and unfortunate ones, just by holding your hands. She felt it now as Inez looked at her sweetly.

"You will be a bride soon, Su-Jin. Your loneliness will disappear."

Inez was right. She had been lonely, terribly lonely all those years, as she slaved away night and day, day and night, working for pennies, below minimum wage, wherever she could, at the jobs that the Americans would not take and she saved little by little, forgoing the invitations from friends for dinner and a movie from time to time, to keep working towards a better life and the solitude of work and work and more work was compounded with the desire to live and prosper in this country and to become a citizen as she taught herself the history of a nation that she dreamed would become her own until the day arrived when she was able to open her little nail and grooming salon in Washington Heights where the rents were cheap and customers plentiful and she would cry herself to sleep at night because of the endless hours and exhaustion and her lonesomeness and fortitude and how her chances for a little family of her own were forever out of her reach as the years went by, one by one, from the life of toil and sacrifice that she had chosen.

"That is what I see Su-Jin as I hold your hand. You will have a very happy life."

Su-Jin kept herself from crying. She was there to comfort Inez.

"Now do you understand, Su-Jin? I see things…and I saw what was going to happen to Lourdes and the others and I could have done something to stop it…but it was too late."

Inez collapsed in Su-Jin's arms as they crossed the vast Bronx graveyard.

"You're just upset, Inez. Come on, let's go home."

Later on, Su-Jin had already gone to Mrs. Dominguez's home to recover Inez's possessions.

"You tell that sin vergüenza that I will not forget what she has done!"

Su-Jin knew that the woman, still upset, was capable of anything. As she hurried down the avenue Su-Jin knew that she would need to work fast to protect Inez. She remembered a friend, someone that she had met through a distant cousin, who owned a little barbecue place in Little Korea.

What was his name?

Yoon-Ling Kim!

Yes, he had recently become a citizen and seemed very knowledgeable about these things with the new immigration laws. Yes, she would speak to him. A very serious man, and attractive, so she recalled.

Her cousin tried to fix them up, but Su-Jin would have none of it. She knew it was too late for her--too late for love.

Although she did admire how Yoon-Ling got along so easily with others and how well he spoke English. He was smart and pleasant, and she knew that he would help. Su-Jin searched her wallet, before boarding the 101 bus, remembering that she had buried his business card away behind the cracking photo of her family in Seoul. "Yoon-Ling Kim, Korean BBQ." Su-Jin flipped the card over.

"Please call me, Su-Jin. Take a chance!"

She had never seen the message before now. She decided to heed his advice.

That night, as soon as they finished their dinner, Su-Jin escorted Inez to a small room near her own bedroom, her thick, graying hair now untied and worn free from the long day.

Inez had never seen Su-Jin with her hair like that.

It made her look young and vibrant.

"This is my sewing room, Inez. For now, you have this fold up mattress, but we will get you a little bed soon, okay?"

Inez sat on the chair near the Singer sewing machine desperate for a good night's sleep.

"Tomorrow I will call my friend. He will help us. I promise you."

Su- Jin felt maternal towards the girl as she did when she first hired Inez at the recommendation of Nilda, a regular customer whom she deeply missed.

"Before I forget, Inez, I have something for you."

Su-Jin left the room as Inez removed one of Nilda's treasured books, a birthday present when she turned seventeen, from her backpack. As she read, she felt her eyes and body give into the exhaustion. She felt safe, at least for now, with Su-Jin.

"I've been wanting to give you this new set of tools, but I never got around to it."

She handed Inez a small tan leather case with a gold zipper that closed all the way around its rectangular body.

"Open it."

Inside Inez found a set of brass coated manicure tools; a nail file, a small cuticle scissors, nail clippers, a nail brush and buffer, that gleamed against the pouch's red velvet lining.

"I found these in a little specialty shop downtown Inez, and I thought you might like them. They're for your own use and you can keep them with you and use them wherever you are."

The set was beautiful, new, and shiny. Inez promised that she would never use it on any of her customers. It would only be for her own hands.

"Now, it's getting late, Inez," said Su-Jin as she dressed the cot for Inez. "We have a lot of work to do tomorrow, ok? Buenas noches."

Su-Jin's Spanish was endearing as Inez laid on the bed and began to dream.

And she saw her parents again and Tio Rafael, in the distance, in the sugar cane fields, on the land that they lived on in El Salvador, calling for her.

"Hija! Hija! Estamos aquí!"

The trio waved happily to Inez as they began to swing their machetes against the wind.

"Mama!"

She wanted to run to them but was paralyzed.

"Hija! Ven acá!"

Inez ran towards them, fighting against the force of wind that seemed to blow from nowhere.

"¡No puedo, mama!"

The trio continued to cut the cane.

The wind began to lift Inez up and away from them.

"Mama!"

Inez looked into her mother's face from way up above from the fields, her round, dark face, upwards and cheerful, each stitch of her clothing colorfully painted in reds and blues, and yellows, bleeding suddenly down her cotton dress, as she wept, and Inez wept, longing to join them as she floated further and further away from them.

"Mama!"

The wind continued to howl as it grew stronger, each gust finally lifting Inez out of sight from her family as they continued to scream for her, leaving behind their machetes in the field, calling for her and never reaching her. Inez woke up and sat up in her bed haunted by the dream, as Su-Jin raced in dressed in her nightgown.

"Someone is knocking, Inez! Get up! Hurry!"

Inez looked at the tiny clock on the sewing machine. It was nearly 6 a.m. She heard men's voices. Low and loud at the same time. She heard Su-Jin speaking as if she was gasping for breath. The men spoke for some time until Su-Jin entered the room.

"I'm sorry, Inez. These men, these terrible, terrible men!"

The two men, dressed in dark blue uniforms with the letters INS emblazoned on the back of their broad shoulders, followed Su-Jin into the tiny room.

"…it must have been Mrs. Dominquez, Inez," Su-Jin continued. "They're here to take you back. Oh, dear little girl, I am so sorry for you! I wanted to talk to my friend Yoon-Ling but it is too late. I'm sorry, Inez."

Inez went over to Su-Jin and gently touched her hair.

Inez thought she was beautiful.

"Su-Jin, remember what I told you? Remember what I said?"

Inez lifted Su-Jin's face towards her.

"You are going to be very happy, Su-Jin, and I will go home."

Su-Jin grabbed Inez and held her in her arms as the men noticeably surveyed the space.

"No funny business, now. Hurry it up!" one of the men jeered.

Inez walked to the closet where just a few hours ago she had unpacked her little valise, somehow knowing that her safety would not last.

"I will do what I can from here, Inez. I promise you. Yoon-Ling and I will help you and your family. Do not worry."

Inez packed everything again and knew that Su-Jin and her future husband's efforts would prove futile.

"Gracias, Su-Jin."

They held each other as the men paced their feet from side to side signaling their impatience.

"It's time to go!"

"I will write to you, Inez. I promise."

But Inez knew that she would never receive Su-Jin's letters and would never again see her or the nail salon or Mrs. Dominguez or America ever again.

One of the agents placed plastic cords around Inez's wrists cutting her with its brittleness.

"Please, don't hurt her! She is just a young girl!"

The imposing man faced the small woman.

"So, where are your papers, Miss…Miss uh…?"

"My name is Su-Jin Sung and I am an American! And this, you, this is not America!" Su-Jin spat out the words causing her thin body to shake with each syllable. "This is not America, Inez!"

"Yeah, yeah, whatever. Come on!"

The men lead Inez towards the door, chained and half asleep.

"I will not forget you, Su-Jin. Que Dios te bendiga!"

"I love you, Inez! We will help you! Yoon-Ling and I! Do not worry!"

Inez tried to reply but the men continued to push her through the door and out into the hallway.

"Come on! They're waiting for you!"

Su-Jin threw herself onto the small mattress aware of what the men meant and who would be waiting for Inez.

"Please God, protect this little angel."

***

The trip back to El Salvador was easy and not as difficult as the one to America. The long flight at least gave her a chance to sleep. Inez awoke as soon as they landed.

The two men, who still accompanied her from New York, had already removed her manacles, secure in knowing that the girl would not jump from a moving aircraft. But as soon as they entered the terminal in San Salvador the men were quick to put them back on.

Inez instantly recognized Father Everett. He had not changed in all those years although he had gained more weight.

"There's no need for those, Officers."

The men shoved an unbound Inez towards the priest.

"You remember me, don't you, dear?" He extended his hand to her.

"Come, we have much to talk about."

Inez resisted. The two men noticed.

"Any trouble, Padre?"

"No, no. I'm sure that once Inez takes my hand she will come along, won't you, Inez?"

Inez stared at the men not wanting to be restrained again with the cutting, hard plastic.

"That's a good girl. Just come along with me."

His hand was wet and cold, as it was before, many years ago. It did not take long for Inez to see what had happened to her family.

Inez wanted to flee, but knew that it would be in vain.

"I need to use…el baño…Padre, por favor."

The men, growing impatient, motioned again for the handcuffs.

"There's no need for that, gentlemen. She needs to use the bathroom. It was a long trip."

Father Everett grinned. She remembered it. It was the same one that he had shown to Enrique before whipping him in the classroom.

"Okay, okay, we'll stand watch outside the door."

The two men led Inez towards the restroom.

"There's always something with these foreigners!"

Inez saw everything as she held Father Everett's hand; her mother, raped and murdered, her body left at the side of a dirt road, her father, wanting to avenge her death, executed before a firing squad, and Tio Rafael and the others who fought with him, discovered inside a little shack near a deserted village, killed mercilessly by the paramilitary death squads with high-powered rifles. And how he would try to use her to kill more, and ultimately her.

They were all gone. Her entire family, slaughtered.

Inez stood in the bathroom, all alone, before one of the mirrors, stifling her tears remembering what her Tio Rafael had promised her, how they would all one day be together again. Inez removed the small leather pouch from her bag. The present from Su-Jin. The grooming tools sat neatly in the case.

Inez reached for the nail file as she moved her hand to her neck, feeling that soft spot just underneath the side of her jaw, remembering that the new file was sharp enough to penetrate steel let alone flesh.

She began to pray for her parents and to ask for God's forgiveness.

She did not want to help Father Everett and those who massacred her family and destroyed her country too.

She knew that she would have to act swiftly in the bathroom before they would also torture and kill her.

Just before she plunged the file into her vein, Inez realized that tomorrow would be her birthday. The drops of blood fell into the stained public basin as she saw her family again, her parents and Tio Rafael, welcoming her from the other side,

"Hola, Inez!" waiting patiently for her arrival and the belated reunion and celebration. "Feliz cumpleaños, Inez!"

And Inez truly knew that never again would she have to break her promise.

Hav-A-Cup
of Coffee

As Doris Day Pierce sifted through the pages and pages of the inventory log, she noticed that ever since Ely hired the new guy, Henry, it seemed like every other week, some kind of coffee supply item was missing.

"Damn! These numbers just don't add up!"

Doris never wanted to get anybody in trouble, since she was once there herself, trouble that is, and she didn't wish it on anyone. Doris fixed the numbers to reflect an even ratio between the number of cans and foil packets of coffee, premium, decaf and regular, the plastic stirrers and spoons, the creamer and sugar, and even the Sweet 'n Low packets on hand with what they actually sold, so that all of it somehow added up and Ely wouldn't get suspicious.

She was good at math, so good that she was just about ready to send out her resume for that accountant position at Citibank, just as soon as she got up the nerve. She had been postponing applying for the job for some time now and she knew that she was more than qualified and made a good candidate, but what held her back was her past. And that was something that she could never escape no matter how hard she tried.

"Doris, I want you to train the new girl."

Ely, her boss, was a saintly man. Doris knew that she and

all of the others would never have been able to find work anywhere else if it wasn't for Ely. He knew that everyone makes mistakes and that everyone deserves a second chance.

"What girl? You didn't tell me about any girl?"

Doris knew how she impressed Ely even from the very start when she first arrived at the midtown coffee supplies distributor nearly ten years ago. Tall, well-groomed and always professionally attired, her manner, her speech, her elegance and articulation never betrayed the fact that she had served time for murder.

"Yes, I did. I told you about her yesterday. The girl from NYU, you know, the student. She'll be here part-time and I want you to show her the ropes."

Ely always trusted Doris and would always look the other way when the numbers didn't quite add up. He knew that she was smart, smarter than anyone he had ever known in his life.

He also knew how she covered for the others. Ely admired her for that. Her nobility. She was loyal and honest and why she served time after defending herself from a rapist who kidnapped and tortured her enraged him with its reprehensible injustice - this made him want to protect and love her even more.

"Oh, yes, now I remember."

Doris removed a file folder from her desk drawer that contained the resumes from the outside world; from the students and interns and bored housewives who needed the extra part-time work.

"Yes, here she is. Isabel Torres, right? Journalism major, minors in English Lit."

Doris was happy that she was able to complete her high

school diploma, Regents with Honors no less, just before her world came to an abrupt end. The judge ruled in favor of the defendant whose lawyer convinced a jury that Doris did not act in self defense, but recklessly and vengefully killed the man who raped and tortured her.

"I majored in English. Looks like we'll have something in common."

Ely picked up the inventory log from her desk.

"These almost done, D? I gotta get everything in by Tuesday."

Doris moved them from his view as she placed them discreetly under her file folder.

"Of course, Ely. You know that I never fail you."

Ely knew she was right. Ten years and not one mistake. He knew that she was bored and unchallenged. She was smart and inventive and all he could give her was a steady paycheck.

No room for growth in his tiny set-up. He wished that he could offer her more but knew that her past was enough to make her a permanent fixture at Hav-A-Cup.

"Ms. Torres will be here at noon and she'll work the afternoon shift. Just give her something to do in the office and then you can show her how to get a delivery ready with the guys."

"Sure thing, Ely."

Doris had worked with other college students in the past. She envied their freedom to be able to get any part-time job that they liked knowing how difficult it was for people like her, and Jerry and Frankie and even the new guy, Henry, to get a minimum wage job through their prisoner reentry programs despite the fact that nearly all of them earned their college degrees behind bars.

She often wondered if these students ever really knew how good they really had it, but she did not spend too much time pondering such thoughts, as she never enjoyed feeling sorry for herself.

Ely returned to his office as Doris looked at the clock, which was in the shape of a coffee cup.

"She'll be here any minute."

Doris rose and walked across the warehouse to where they kept all the supplies. She found Jerry sitting with Henry, the new guy, in the employee's lunch area busily picking his nails clean with a pair of scissors.

"Please put those away, Jerry. Makes me nervous."

Jerry always wore a thick, plaid jacket and a black, wool knit cap over his head, even when it was warm out. He always had a blank look in his eyes that he had acquired while serving time. But he was a hard worker, one of the best in the stockroom, although sometimes his past got the best of him.

"Hi, Doris, how are you? I can see from your aura that you need to drink some orange juice."

Doris waved her hand at him, dismissing the wild notion with her perfectly manicured hands.

"Jerry, what did I tell you about that? None of that hocus-pocus talk around the students, ok?"

Jerry removed a tiny carton of Tropicana orange juice from his pocket and held it up for Doris.

"I know that it can get a little frustrating for you, Doris. You gotta learn to shake it off. Here, drink this. Are we getting a new student?"

Doris carefully inspected the stockroom picking up the

small packets of artificial sweetener and Domino sugar that littered its floor.

"Where's Frankie? I want him to meet the new student. He can show her how to assemble a delivery."

Jerry opened the tiny carton and began to drink.

"He's late again. He called to say that he had to take his son to the doctor's."

"That's the third time in two weeks. As soon as he gets in, Jerry, please have him see me."

Jerry sipped noisily from the container.

"Here, Doris. I left you some juice."

Doris gently patted his arm, looking into his eyes, searching for some lucidity.

"That's okay, Jer. You drink it for me. I'm trying to watch my figure."

A tall woman, nearly 5'10", Doris knew that she needed to lose at least ten pounds before she booked that cruise to the Bahamas with her cousin in June. The trip was one that she had been planning now for almost six months. The prospect of leaving the country, let alone the city, was both exhilarating and nerve-racking having never done either one in her entire life.

The sun, the ocean, the town and the new people; another dream that seemed to be within reach but still a dream nonetheless.

"Okay, Doris, cool. I'll send Frankie over when he gets in. Come on, Henry, let's get back to work."

The two men disappeared into the stock room as Jerry lectured Henry about the benefits of vitamin C. Doris raced back to her office knowing that the new student would soon arrive as she made a mental note to speak with Frankie about his two-year-old son.

Doris knew how much he adored his son despite the mistake he made with the boy's mother - he was a devoted father and took his responsibilities seriously.

"Hello, I'm Isabel. I'm here about the job."

Her voice was so tiny that Doris almost mistook it for a child's.

"I'm a little early but I wanted to get a good start."

She carried a large backpack that was slung around her right arm and probably weighed more than she. Khaki trousers, a plain white shirt and shiny maroon penny loafers, were her outfit, and she wore her hair in a ponytail. She acted and looked professional. Doris liked that.

"Hello, my name is Doris. Doris Pierce. Come on in, Ms. Torres, and have a seat.'

"Thank you, Ms. Pierce."

"Please call me Doris."

"And I am Isabel."

Doris sat opposite her and opened the file folder.

"Well, I see that you're a journalism student. Any plans after graduation?"

It was the question that she not only enjoyed asking but also detested at the same time.

Had things been different she would not have had to earn her BA inside a prison. Had things been different she would have gone instead to a college in upstate New York and lived on campus rather than at a correctional facility for women. Had things been different she would have traveled to Europe after graduation and spent at least a year abroad experiencing life and different cultures rather than pulling laundry duty and sleeping endless nights, months and years inside a locked cage. Had things been different.

Isabel sighed loudly and shifted uncomfortably in her seat. "I don't know. I'm not sure if I can get a job as a reporter right after school. I applied for something part-time at a newspaper and another time at one of the news networks and they made me take a typing test. They wouldn't even look at my journalism portfolio. So, this was the only thing available."

Isabel realized that she was offensive without meaning to be. "I mean, um, what I mean is, that uh, when I found out that this company caters to hundreds of offices throughout the city... "Isabel tried to explain away her ignorance, embarrassed by her stupidity. "I knew that it would be a really interesting and exciting opportunity for me."

Doris knew that she was lying, like the other students before her, who needed the extra cash for books and God knows what else. She took no offense at the slight. Ely was always a generous man to all, especially to college kids and ex-offenders.

"Yes, I understand. Come on. Let me show you around and introduce you to some of the guys."

"Thank you, Ms. Pierce. This means a lot to me." Isabel knew that she was right about that.

She was still living with her parents and the extra cash would come in handy for her school supplies and carfare and lunches and even the dinners when she had to stay late at the library.

Her parents were poor, and with Pa sick and Mami making pennies at the factory, to ask for even a dollar from them was more than she could bear.

"I told you, Isabel. It's Doris."

Isabel immediately noticed how large her hands were, almost manly, which contrasted with the neat little bun of hair that sat firmly on the top of her head, tightly wound with an elaborate colorful orange nylon bow that complimented her creamy, molasses skin. Her pencil skirt and pink blouse also conveyed a sort of femininity and grace, which contrasted with her height, which Isabel figured, was at least 6 feet.

"We supply ground coffee and instant coffee, as well as all the supplies, paper cups, creamers, plastic stirrers, sugar, diet sweeteners, everything and anything that an office might need in order to brew a fresh cup of coffee in the morning. We even sell them to the brewers. Jerry, come here. I want to introduce you to somebody."

Jerry had already finished cleaning his fingernails, still wearing the black wool hat that covered his receding hairline.

"Jerry, this is our new office assistant Isabel. She'll help out back here with getting deliveries ready and help me in the office with our accounts. Isabel, this is Jerry."

Jerry gripped her hand into his, holding it still, barely shaking it as he spoke.

"I can see that you're anxious, Isabel. You better remember to drink some orange juice in the morning so that anxiety can go away."

Isabel let go of the man's strong hand.

She had been anxious for some time, about Pa's illness and the pressures of school; regular panic attacks that seemed to jump out of nowhere at any given moment.

"Just take it easy young lady. You're young. You got a

whole life ahead of you."

Doris looked at Isabel and shrugged her shoulders.

"Okay, that's enough, Jerry. Where's Frankie?"

"Here I am!"

The tall, young good looking man swayed his hips from side to side as he moved towards them.

"Sorry I'm late Doris, but my son, Jason, got sick again and you know how lazy his mother is and then by the time we got to the doctor's office it was packed! We waited almost two hours before that doctor saw us! Hi, I'm Frankie."

He held out his hand as if it was to be kissed.

"I'm Isabel."

"Pleased to meet you, honey. I like your shoes."

"Thanks."

Doris cleared her throat as she tried to push Isabel back into the front office.

"I'm showing Isabel around Frankie and then I want you to show her how to fill the orders. What are those for?"

Frankie lowered his sunglasses to reveal a fresh bruise that encircled his left eye.

"Just another little 'love tap' from Richie."

Doris knew that this new assault was a pattern of abuse that Frankie had endured since meeting Richie over a year ago.

Since it began Frankie would walk in with either a new pair of sunglasses, the darkest ones he can find, or at least a pound of pancake makeup to conceal the beatings.

Doris knew about these things; violence and how it happened in the home. She knew where it might lead to, and where it took her, inside a tiny cell, and she didn't want that for Frankie. Not again.

Frankie was a good father. Yes, he made some mistakes, years ago when he was picked up for selling an ounce of pot and got ten years for it. But at least he came to work each and every single day. And yes, she knew that he would steal some of the small packets of coffee and sugar when he thought no one was looking but that was okay because she knew how hard it was to support his young son and the boy's mother, who was trying to get off crack. Frankie even went to school at night to get his GED. But then he met Richie.

"Reckless Richie" is what Jerry called him when he first met him and Doris thought it fit him to a T.

She knew his type, the controlling, angry type, who would go into a rage at the drop of a hat for no particular reason at all; the littlest thing would set him off, and Doris saw it in him - the frenzy in his eyes; it was a familiar danger. "What do I keep telling you about that guy, Frankie?"

"Yeah, I know that he's no good for me, Doris. But you know how it is with guys who have big dicks!"

Doris furrowed her brow as she glanced at Isabel. Embarrassed for her and herself.

"Sorry, Doris. I didn't know that we had Mary Poppins here."

"Well, if I'm Mary Poppins then you must be the Wicked Bitch of the West."

Doris was impressed. Isabel could take care of herself.

"Ooh, did you hear that? This girl got some mouth." Frankie faced Isabel.

"I didn't mean nothing by it, ok? Just stating the obvious. I mean, I like my men big!"

Frankie laughed as Jerry hovered nearby.

"Big men, Frankie. They're no good for you, man. You better start drinking that orange juice 'cause you're gonna need your energy against that big man."

"Oh, shush, Jerry! You don't know what you're talking about."

Frankie walked towards Isabel and locked his arm into hers.

"You know I love working with you college kids. They add a little class to this dump!"

Jerry looked at Doris defeated by the remarks.

"Don't worry Doris, he didn't mean it. He's just a little stressed right now."

"That's okay, Jer."

"He's gotta be careful though. That big man drinks a lot more orange juice than Frankie and he's stronger and bigger and he…he…"

Doris knew that Jerry lost his mind in prison, having spent most of his youth as pickpocket and petty thief, in and out of foster homes. A hold-up at a bank, years later, was enough to put him away for nearly 15 years. Doris knew that he paid his dues and then some.

"He what, Jerry?"

She also knew when to listen to him. She listened when he spoke now; in that low, hushed tone that she learned to pay full attention to while in prison.

"Tell me Jerry. Do you think Richie is gonna hurt Frankie?"

Jerry waved her off as he retreated back into the stockroom to help Henry.

"There's nothing more to say, Doris. I already told him

that he needs more orange juice!"

Both Doris and Ely knew that Jerry was growing increasingly more scattered, his thoughts more and more fractured, reflecting a state of a mind that was beyond help. But they couldn't get rid of him and lose him again to the system. Jerry, despite his lunacy, was there forever. He was family.

Doris caught up with Isabel and Frankie in the front office.

"So, have you shown Isabel a little of our bookkeeping system, Frankie?"

Frankie and Isabel were chatting amicably near Doris' corner desk.

"Not really, Doris. Isabel's been telling me about some of her classes at NYU. I told her that once I pass my GED I'm gonna take my little behind over to that college of hers and become a college student!"

Doris sat at her desk as she shooed them both away like tiny banana flies.

"Frankie, it's gonna take a lot more work than just registering. You have to take the SATs, right Isabel? And then if you score well, you have to complete the application for admissions and then after that…

Isabel sat in the chair opposite. "And after that you wait," she interrupted. "But if you have good scores, Frankie, I'm sure you can get into any school that you want."

Frankie glowed as if he had just won the Mega Millions jackpot. "Really, you really think so? Any school? You mean I can apply to, like, Yale or Harvard or some school like that?"

"I don't see why not. And you have something that I

didn't have, Frankie. You have life experience."

Isabel noticed Doris twitching nervously in her chair.

"You know, you're not the average student and a lot of schools really dig that."

Isabel swayed absentmindedly in her seat. "Sometimes I wished I had taken that route instead of going straight from high school into college. You know, like, take a break like you guys. Live life, get experience and then go to school. Right now, school is such a drag. My professors are so boring."

Doris had seen this before. If only Isabel knew of their so-called "life experience."

"So you don't like school, eh?"

Doris never understood this. She just couldn't understand how these students just wasted it all away.

The opportunity. The freedom.

"No, it's not that, Doris, it's just that, I don't know, I guess I'm just lonely. NYU is tough to make friends because everyone is a commuter. It's hard."

Doris understood loneliness. She had it since she was 18 for 20 long, hard years. And she knew, deep down, how it hardened her. She saw it each morning in the mirror when she woke, her face once so full of hope now profoundly frozen, carved into an iron, invisible mask, molded by the years of solitude and bitterness of a life behind bars.

When she looked at photos of herself in her teens before it all happened, she wondered how she would ever become herself again. She knew that it was impossible.

"Well, I understand how you can feel lonely. But don't worry, you stay here with us and soon you'll have more than enough friends. I see that you and Frankie are already bosom buddies."

Frankie flirtatiously pulled Isabel's seat towards him.

"Girl…you just stick with me, and I'll show you how to have fun!"

Doris knew that they had a lot of orders to fill that day.

"That's enough goofing off, Frankie. Show Isabel how we take the orders and issue an account number and how we log everything into the books and then at three you can take a break and…"

Isabel knowingly smiled.

"Wait, don't tell me, *hav-a-cup of coffee*, right?"

Doris returned the smile although she didn't really want to.

"Not really, we also have tea, if you're into that. Come on - it's getting late and if Ely comes back and finds out that I didn't train you properly he'll pull one of his hissy fits and believe you me, that's nothing that you'd ever want to witness."

All three sat together at the small desk as Doris showed Isabel how to balance the books.

"Sometimes it's a little off, but we don't tell Ely about it."

Frankie was late again that next morning as Doris had already called Isabel to help them with a large order.

"Thanks for getting here on such short notice but we have a huge delivery to prepare for our new corporate client. We could really use the extra hand."

"Where's Frankie?"

Doris looked at Ely. She did her best to cover up Frankie's recent lateness and bruises as best as she could but she was running out of excuses.

"It's his son, again, Ely. That little boy has more ear infections than you have fingers. It's normal, I think, and since Frankie's the responsible parent, he's the only one who can take him to the doctor."

Doris had no other choice but to lie. She didn't like to do that to Ely. He didn't deserve it.

She had not heard from Frankie at all that morning, which was very unusual for him as he was always quick to call, even before dawn, in the event of an emergency.

"You know, I think they got some kind of, uh, new kinda, uh, surgery for those things. Maybe you should let Frankie know."

"Sure, Ely."

Doris remembered what Jerry had said and hoped that his premonition would not come to pass.

"Jerry, Henry! Come with me in the van and we'll take these over. Doris, please call the client and tell them that we're on our way. Thank you Isabel, you saved the day for Hav-A-Cup!"

They hurried off as Doris and Isabel went into the small office.

"I'm worried about Frankie, Isabel."

Doris picked up the receiver as she dialed.

"Something awful happened. I can feel it in my bones. No answer!"

"Maybe we can go over there, Doris, maybe we can go to his house and see if he's okay."

All at once, Frankie came in struggling with the door screaming.

"Help me, Doris! Help me! He's comin' after me!" Frankie

collapsed in her arms.

"He kept me in the house, Doris. He wouldn't let me leave, that's why I couldn't come in. My sister came to pick up Jason and then he went ballistic on me. I tried. I tried to make him stop but he kept hitting on me, Doris…"

Frankie cried openly into Doris's heaving chest. "I tried to stop him, Doris, but he wouldn't. Please help me, Doris."

Isabel ran into the restroom returning with wet hand towels. Doris comforted him in her arms as she felt that familiar heat rising within; the same heat that swelled from deep inside her as the anger returned, the memory of her own assault and now Frankie, melting into one, both victims of violent men.

"Don't worry, dear, everything will be alright. I'm not gonna let him touch you, Frankie. I will not allow this to happen again."

Isabel pressed against Frankie's wounds to soak up the bleeding.

"What do you mean, Doris? Did this happen before? I don't understand…"

Doris knew that she needed to calm Isabel and take care of Frankie at the same time.

"All of us here, Isabel, we've all been in jail, we're all ex-convicts…"

"Oh, D, it hurts, it hurts."

Doris worried that the injuries were internal as well.

"We still all have dreams, Isabel, me and Frankie and even Jerry with all his craziness. We've made mistakes but we paid the price and then some."

"I don't understand, Doris. Is Frankie okay? Is he gonna

be okay? Maybe I should call the police…?"

Isabel rose as Doris continued to cradle the young man in her arms.

"No one's going to hurt you now Frankie."

Isabel noticed Richie first as she walked towards the restroom to get more towels as well as the gun that he carried.

"Doris!"

Doris held Frankie tighter to her bosom, unrelenting in her protection of her friend.

"Go to the office, Isabel. Close the door and call the police! Now!"

Isabel ran towards the room still carrying the bloodied paper towels.

"You come one step closer, Richie and you're going to be in big trouble. Don't be stupid."

Richie pointed the gun at them, while aiming at Frankie.

"Shut up bitch! Who you think you talking to? Get up Frankie!"

Frankie clutched at Doris, frantic.

"Don't let him kill me, Doris! Don't let him hurt me!"

Frankie's cries sank deeply into her heart and her memories of fighting for her own life many years ago. Doris noticed that Frankie's shirt was now completely covered in blood.

She was right about the internal damage. Doris placed Frankie behind her using herself as his shield.

"I'm warning you, Richie, take one more step and…"

The gun blast sounded more like a Fourth of July firecracker that she would often hear from her window at night even when it wasn't the Fourth of July.

"Fuck you, bitch!"

The man fired again as Doris stood leaving Frankie on the floor. She stumbled towards the man, with the first bullet now lodged in her heart, holding out her two hands, wanting him to stop.

"Bitch!"

He shot at her again as Doris fell to one knee still with her arms raised high against the assault.

"No!"

Frankie lunged at Richie as he weakly unleashed a fury of punches and kicks.

"No! No more! No more, Richie, please!"

The police sirens rang outside as Frankie tried to disarm the man.

"Please, Richie, stop! Stop!"

Isabel returned to the scene as the two men continued to brawl.

"Doris!"

Doris remembered feeling the first bullet enter her, almost wishing that it was a mosquito bite. And then the other, ripping her insides in the stomach area as she could actually feel the exploding gunpowder within darkening her light as she began to fall, fall, fall, into the widening gap between her present life and her past, appearing to her again, when she was a girl, happy with her parents, and then the man that she knew from the neighborhood who invited her for a soda that turned into something else, something sinister, that she had no other choice than to defend herself with the pen that she carried around in her pocket to write the lines of poetry that would come to her in those quiet moments on the train or on the bus, and how she found it and used it, as a weapon to protect herself after he raped her and beat her, as the blood continued to ruin her favorite blouse, the one that she wanted to take with her to the Bahamas, feeling its tackiness against her flesh, wanting to push the silk away from her damaged body, wanting to excise the deadly pieces of metal now wedged deeply within and inside her dreams and her plans, and she saw Isabel coming closer to her as the police raced in, separating Frankie from the murderer, handcuffing Richie, as Isabel turned to Frankie, tending to his wounds, while at the same time saying something to her, "hang in there Doris," "don't leave us, please," as she fought to remain there with them and not pay attention to the images of her prison cell, trapped, alone, wrongly convicted of saving her own life, as her parents wept, and as hard as she tried, she couldn't hang in there anymore and she couldn't stop the bleeding, and she knew that her life meant nothing, even with all her dreams, as she saw Ely kneeling, holding her, weeping over her, like a devoted father, "Doris, don't leave us, dear, dear, Doris, my poor girl, my poor girl," and she saw Isabel carry Frankie away from the scene with Jerry, happy that they were friends and drinking orange juice, and she thought that maybe Isabel would help Frankie to make all his dreams come true, and she knew finally that this was for the best after all, ending it all there at Hav-A-Cup, where at least she was given a chance to dream, even for a little while. And she saw them approaching her, hand in hand, like she remembered just before she was locked up, her Mom and Dad, looking lovingly at her, finally reunited with their only child, and she saw herself, dressed in her favorite blue jeans and white cotton shirt, in her senior year at school just before the man crushed her world, and she rose from Ely's arms, and ran towards the Bahamian Sun that was her parents and she was happy, finally happy, as if nothing had ever happened.

THE MAN WHO DREAMED TOO MUCH

Eddie Rios was in love with a woman who would not love him back.

That is, Dalliancia De Jesus could not love him.

"I never promised you anything Eddie," she would explain to him for the millionth time that week and whenever they would meet at their secret favorite spot, El Coqui, just a mile away from the little mobile phone store that she owned with her husband on Vermilyea.

Eddie shoveled more sugar into his coffee as he stared at her. He admired how she wore her hair up, because of the city's heat, and tucked into place by the millions of black bobby pins that glided around her scalp resembling a trail of bumpy, wart headed crocodiles. He sipped his coffee in silence as she stared at him, pleading with him to understand. Eddie swallowed the hot liquid with difficulty, embittered by the taste of the drink and her words, injured by his foolishness to fall in love with a married woman.

But he could not contain his passion for her, not even from the very first moment when he saw her in the cell phone store where he picked up an earpiece last summer.

He recalled how she would greet each customer with a graciousness that transcended that of any mortal being. He knew that he had instantly placed her on par with the angels that would often accompany his past dreams about his dead parents.

She was indeed a sight to behold despite the obvious weight gain from having two children, and the over use of a lip liner that framed her already naturally full brown lips.

Everyone loved her.

Men admired her curves, which fitted neatly into her low cut jeans and the women customers always took note of how she'd always look them in the eye first and never addressed their men directly; it was a sign of respeto and they liked that from the dark beauty.

She was a whole woman, una mujer entera, as they would say.

Eddie poured more sugar into the boiling cup and closed his eyes. From where he sat he could even smell the tiny dabs of Obsession perfume that she'd dot behind each of her earlobes.

Even these small amounts would torture him, increasing the hurt between his legs, the longing for her in his heart, in his arms.

"I know you never promised anything, D, but I'm getting tired of waiting."

Eddie was growing impatient for her, waiting for things to change with her situation at home. The wait would leave him feeling hopeless and utterly alone.

Dalliancia knew this.

She began to wonder if perhaps she had made an error that afternoon, almost a year ago, when she said "hello" to the tall guapo, UPS delivery man who had come into her store to buy an earpiece for his cell phone.

She and Orlando, her devoted and unknowing husband,

had opened the store a few years earlier. They were paying their overhead and even managed to make a little profit by day's end. They even decided to add on a Western Union to accommodate the ever-growing immigrant population in the neighborhood who would send their earnings back home.

Things were going well for them.

Their success with the store even brought her and Orlando closer, as the extra income bought them extra time together with their two daughters and less stress about the unending bills.

But she knew that there was something missing.

It was the excitement that always accompanied new love; the love that now hissed its way out of their inflating prosperity, deflating itself from their intimacy like the slow, sad sighs that would often greet her mornings and end her nights.

It was because of this that Dalliancia noticed Eddie as soon as he walked in; a tall, young, bronzed man with dark, shiny hair, a strong physique and a nice butt. She would often see him delivering packages in the area, with his partner, a young Afro-Americana named Jennie. But that afternoon Eddie was alone and he carried no packages. That afternoon, Dalliancia knew, deep down, that Eddie was there for more than just an earpiece.

"Hola, Dalliancia. How are you today?"

His face was one that remained inside her memories when she closed the store late that night after Orlando had left to pick up the kids from the after-school center on Fort Washington Avenue. And for some reason, quite out of nowhere, whether she was storing away some freshly arrived cell phones or whether she was in the middle of assisting a customer with the mechanics of wiring cash through the wireless system, she would think of Eddie, just out of nowhere, and how his essence made her feel tingly and good, all at once, renewing a forgotten excitement.

"I'm fine, Eddie. What can I do for you today?"

She saw it. And she recognized it. How he would stare deeply into her eyes, shy but growing more and more intense with each weekly visit. She was enchanted by his allure and the obvious attraction to her, to the point where ultimately, all she could do was to return it in kind.

Eventually they would meet secretly and later, as their intimacy grew, would even sneak off to a motel in the Bronx in East Tremont when they had the chance. But usually they would meet here, in the tiny restaurant, far enough away from the store and suspicious eyes.

"Listen, Eddie, maybe we should stop seeing each other."

At once, Eddie's soul cracked; he could almost hear its rupture.

"I don't think that I can do this anymore, all this hiding and sneaking around. Nobody is really hidden, Eddie, nobody. Even God sees what we're doing."

Eddie knew that Dalliancia was religious but this was the first time that she had interjected guilt into their love.

"God? What you think is gonna happen, D? Like we're gonna go to hell or something just because we love each other?"

Dalliancia turned away from him as she began to fuss with her purse. Eddie already knew her. She was hiding something, something that she didn't really want to discuss.

"You do love me, D, right?

Her silence was resolute and puzzling.

"D, please, you're just afraid, that's all…."

He reached for her arm, touching it as if she were made of stardust.

"Please, Eddie. It has nothing to do with love." Dalliancia moved to exit the restaurant. "You're living in a dream world, Eddie. I can't give you anything!"

"Your love, D. Isn't that enough?"

"No, Eddie, not enough for you. It's not fair. Tengo una familia, Eddie. I love them. I won't leave them."

Eddie walked towards her and knelt on the floor right there in the diner.

"But we can work things out, D. You don't love Orlando. We can take the girls and, and…"

"And what? And what? Get up! You look stupid!"

Her sharp words smacked him as if she had swatted away an annoying mosquito.

"I love my husband, Eddie. I love him, too."

"I don't understand…"

Dalliancia took his hand and sat him back down into the chair, speaking to him in motherly tones.

"I can't give my love to only you, Eddie, to only Orlando and the girls, I love you all. But they are my family…"

"But we can be a family, D…just the other night I dreamed that."

"Eddie! Pobre Eddie! Wake up! Listen to me! I have nothing to give. Nothing to give…to you."

Dalliancia hurried towards the restaurant's cashier, nervously removing the leaves of crumpled cash from her purse.

"Listen I got a lot of work to do, Eddie. I gotta do some inventory and still have to make it to the bank before three."

Eddie sat still in the chair, growing weaker and weaker in the realization that his dreams of them evaporated, stomped out by her inflammatory words.

"And I'm sure Jennie must be waiting for you in the truck. I don't want you guys to get into any more trouble." Eddie knew Dalliancia was right about that.

Day after day, it grew increasingly difficult to wake up from his dreams of her. His beautiful dreams of holding her and being with her forever. The dreams caused him to remain asleep, missing his early deliveries with Jennie. Shoot! If it weren't for Jennie, who'd always cover for him, he'd be out of a job by now.

Jennie, whenever she got her chance, would warn him about it and everything else for that matter.

"Yo, man, it ain't none of my business but she's married and to me, man, that means nothing but trouble. It's even affecting your job, man. How many times have I had to save your ass because you're too busy sleeping and dreaming about her and not getting up in time for your shift, uh?" Eddie knew that Jennie was right.

As time passed, though he and D grew closer, he felt like they would never be together. The only place where he found hope was in his dreams of her; when he would finally go to sleep and feel her there in his arms, in their lives together. It was bliss and he'd never want to wake up, he'd never want to face the harsh reality of not being able to be with her 24/7. It was too much for his heart to bear.

A reality without her. So, why not dream?

Why not get lost in his fantasies of her? Who was it harming?

Although he now knew that he could probably lose his job for it and maybe even one day will himself never to awake, he didn't care. As long as he was with her, that was all that mattered, even if it was just in his dreams.

But Eddie knew Jennie was right about everything. He vowed to convince D that they should run away together, finally and once and for all.

Eddie slowly rose from the stifling booth's vinyl seat as he followed Dalliancia out of the diner.

"Can I call you later, D?"

Dalliancia wanted to ignore the request as she feigned an interest to find something inside her bag; maybe some peace of mind.

"What?"

Eddie knew that their days would always end like this; and lately it happened more and more.

Was he being selfish to expect that the woman that he loved would give it all up for him? That perhaps his dreams would come true?

As the days wasted away into weeks then months, he knew that one day he would have to settle for her truth.

"Nothing, D. I'll speak to you soon."

Dalliancia did not dare to look away from her empty purse as she tried to hail a cab.

Her love, at times, for Eddie frightened her as she wondered whether to give in to those impulses and hop into the next taxi with Eddie, head to the airport where they would fly off together, at last, to the Dominican Republic or Puerto Rico or even Mexico, where she would get a quickie divorce and end it all with Orlando and ask for her children to join her and Eddie in their new home in los campos where they would begin their new lives together and harvest coffee beans and sugarcane and plant their vegetables and live the life that she longed for, that she now missed, the happy home on her island, where despite their poverty they would be happy, truly happy.

"Okay, Eddie. Take care."

The words came out of her throat like pieces of jagged glass, the untruth cutting her insides.

He opened the car's door as it sped away leaving a trace of her penetrable scent.

Eddie walked towards his UPS truck, parked over on Nagle, finding it empty, knowing that Jennie was either making a final delivery or was busy with lunch.

"Oh, shit!"

Eddie noticed what resembled a parking ticket hanging from the car's windshield. "Damn it! Not another one!"

"Need spiritual advice?"
"Need spiritual healing?"
"Call 1-800-2-SUEÑOS for a free consultation!"

"Yo, man! Sorry I'm late! But I had to wait for them to let me in the building on 204th. Yo, man you okay? Shit! Is that another ticket?"

Eddie handed Jennie the advertisement as they hurried into the truck.

"Nah, man, just some stuff about dreams. Put your seatbelt on Jen. This might be the 'hood but these cops are still hungry to fill their quota!"

Jennie locked herself safely in as Eddie thought about what Dalliancia had told him.

He knew that she was lying about how she felt but he knew that she was right about what she had to do.

"Yo, man, says here you can get a free consultation. You're always talking about those dreams of yours man. Why don't you go see this guy? See what he has to say."

"Shit, man, I ain't into any of that voodoo stuff and anyway D already told me that she didn't want to see me anymore, that it's too complicated. She fucking broke up with me, man. Why can't it be easy, man? Just like in my dreams?" Jennie returned the small flyer.

"I'm sorry, Ed, I truly am, but maybe it's for the best, man. I'm worried about you. All you wanna do is go home and go to sleep and have those dreams about that girl. That ain't no way to live, man, you can't live sleeping! That's like dying!"

Eddie stepped on the brakes abruptly jolting them both forward in their seats.

"It's my life, Jen! It's *my* dream! If I wanna spend it sleeping and dreaming about Dalliancia then I will. For the rest of my life if I have to! Even if she leaves me. I don't care! It's my fucking life!"

Jennie adjusted herself and settled back into the seat ensuring that her long braids were still safely tucked under her UPS cap.

"Man, you brake like that again, I'm gonna have to take

over, understand?"

Eddie lightly stepped on the gas and proceeded towards the end of their day's shift.

"Sorry, Jen."

"Listen, Ed, you're my best friend, I'm just looking out for you. Whether it's some voodoo guy or maybe even a shrink, you gotta talk to somebody, somebody who can set you right, so you ain't sleeping your life away, that's all."

They drove past Dalliancia's little shop just as Orlando was returning with the girls from their after-school program.

Eddie's van passed the store noticing the family's intimacy.

It made him terribly sad.

"Let me see that flyer."

At the stop sign Eddie stared at the trio, smiling and laughing, as they entered the store and he saw D, running towards them, holding them, including Orlando, and he realized in that moment that she would never be able to hold him like that.

"1-800-2- SUEÑOS…I don't know, Jen…"

"Give it a shot man, maybe he can help you at least start dreaming about something else now that you two broke up. Come on, it's time to close shop and I gotta get ready for my date with Caridad."

As Jennie confirmed her plans on her cell phone, Eddie noticed that the spiritualist lived at the projects on West 103rd and Amsterdam, only a few stops from his apartment.

Jennie loudly snapped closed her flip phone.

"I'm all set with my baby."

As the truck drove away from Dalliancia's store Jennie placed her arm on Eddie's shoulder.

"Forget about her, Ed. You'll find someone else."

But he knew that Jennie was wrong. Dalliancia was irreplaceable.

"Let's get the fuck outta here."

Eddie sped off as soon as the light went green knowing that he needed to do something to get over Dalliancia even if it killed him.

Upon arriving at the address from the flyer Eddie rang the building's intercom system bell for some time until he finally heard the faint voice coming through the speaker from apartment 16-H.

"Hi, uh, my name is Eddie. I saw your ad…and…"

The buzzer's rusty timbre activated the door.

Eddie entered the lobby already littered with the day's coming and goings of the residents in the public housing complex; candy wrappers, supermarket circulars ripped in half, the ever-present odor of marijuana that the kids smoked in the stairwell and a small crowd of people already assembled waiting for the stalled elevators.

"Well, looks like something's going on the 5th floor, might as well walk up," announced an old man, a resident, who walked feebly and carried two large bags filled with groceries.

"Well, this is gonna be my exercise for the day," he sadly rationalized. "Anybody wanna join me?"

Eddie was tired from the day and didn't look forward to climbing the 16 flights but at least he could help the man along the way with his packages.

"Look! It's coming!"

The small crowd moved as one, inching closer to the elevator.

"Better hurry in before this one gets stuck too."

Eddie was the last one to disembark as the heavy, industrial green, steel door noisily closed behind him. Would this be his last stop?

Would this be his last chance to finally forget about D without having to sleep his life away?

He heard the man's frail voice from behind the closed door.

"I'm coming…"

The man cracked open the door revealing a sliver of himself behind the door's chain lock that swung between them.

"Hi, I'm Eddie. I saw your ad…and…"

Eddie held up the ad as the man closed the door and slid the chain away from its latch.

"Yes, yes, come in, come in."

The door seemed to move in slow motion as Eddie could already sense that he was entering a different realm, one not belonging to the projects at all.

"Come in, and please take off your shoes before entering. You are now on sacred ground."

In the foyer, Eddie removed his Reeboks in the dimmed light.

"My name is Joaquin Verde. But you can call me Jack. Please come in."

The friendly man led Eddie into the living room as Eddie immediately took him in: of average height, an elderly man but possessing the exaggerated muscular body of a body builder or an ex-con—there was not one wrinkle on his taut, gleaming charcoal skin. And he was toothless!

"Ha! I already see it in your eyes! It's a woman isn't it? It's a woman who is causing you this trouble and she is what brings you here to me, isn't it? Isn't it?" the man cackled.

Eddie noticed that his bald head shone like a polished globe, ominous and almost comical.

The room was nearly bare except for a hefty size combination weight-training machine, complete with pulleys and thick barbells.

There were no paintings on the whitewashed walls except for one wall that was completely covered with full-length mirrors.

"This is where I work out. Y'know gotta keep those muscles strong."

The old man wore a red ribbed sleeveless t-shirt and faded black sweatpants having obviously finished a session.

"You never know when you gotta come to someone's rescue." The man winked at Eddie as he retreated to another room. "Stay here, make yourself at home and I'll be right back."

Eddie settled into the lone chair, a battered brown suede recliner, as the man instantly returned, almost as if he never left.

"By the way, this is just a formality and please don't take any offense. I mean, I can tell by your cute little brown shorts and shirt that you're a UPS guy but I really need to see some ID I'm sorry. I need to be careful, especially these days."

The man's apology endeared him to Eddie, who had grown used to delivering packages to wary residents in the city, who by instinct never trusted anyone in a uniform.

"Yeah, yeah sure, here."

Jack held the photo ID up and close to Eddie's face comparing the two.

"Eddie, Eddie Rios. Yep, that's you all right. Here. I'll be right back."

Before returning his ID back inside his wallet Eddie noticed the strip of black and white snapshots that he and Dalliancia took of themselves at one of those automated photo booths in Coney Island last summer while Orlando and the girls were in the Dominican Republic.

Eddie unfolded the tiny squares of images, five in the strip, of them clowning around and holding each other in front of the quick flashing camera.

How he wished that he would be able to be as comfortable and free in front of the world with D without fear every single waking day.

"So, that's her, right?"

Jack returned with a tall glass of water filled with ice cubes.

"Here. Thought you might need that. It's been a long hot day. I got mine here."

Jack retrieved a plastic bottle near his exercise machine.

"Gotta keep the body hydrated, Eddie. You never know where you'll end up where there's nothing but sand to drink."

Eddie returned the strip of photos into his wallet wondering what the hell Jack referred to as he sipped the drink.

"So, tell me, Eddie, Eddie, right? What can I do for you?"

Eddie squirmed. "Well, you see Mister Verde…"

"Please call me Jack."

The man drank loudly from the container. Eddie noticed

the girth of his arm muscles, impressed by the man's devotion to exercise despite his age.

"Jack… I found this on my windshield and my buddy, Jennie, you know she's my partner at work, well, she thought it might be a good idea…"

Jack continued to drink as Eddie began to notice that the water never seemed to diminish; it was as if the water replenished itself magically after each one of Jack's enthusiastic gulps.

Or maybe it was just his imagination.

Jack returned the bottle to its place near the base of the machine.

"So, your friend, uh? She wanted you to come and see me?"

Eddie nervously crossed his legs and began to tap his right foot in the air thinking that maybe he had made a mistake about seeing the old kook.

"Yeah, well, after thinking about it, I thought it might be good to at least talk to someone, a shrink or a counselor…or someone…"

"Someone, like me? A psychic? A soothsayer? An analyst? What do you think it is that I do, Eddie?"

The man moved to the window.

"There's a bit of a breeze Eddie, especially when the sun goes down, right about this time. You feel that?"

The slight wind embraced Eddie's heart, cooling its heat and anxiety about Dalliancia.

"I don't know what you do, Mister…I mean Jack…but your ad says that you can help people and that's why I'm here. I need your help."

Jack stood before Eddie and motioned for him to rise.

"Come to the back, Eddie. Into my office. Don't worry I won't bite."

Eddie followed the man down a short hallway surprised by his own immediate trust of the stranger. They passed a small kitchen on the way that looked like any ordinary kitchen, with a small round dining table and two chairs.

"Right in here."

Eddie could already feel the room's electricity even before Jack opened the door.

Its energy was visceral with its smells of incense and fragrant candles and from its collective air of mediation and solitude.

The room contained a sort of ottoman and a small wooden stool as well as a table upon which laid various icons including some that his mother had around the house: Ochosi's bow and arrow inside Ogun's large iron cauldron, and the little Esu that she placed near their door.

Unlike the living room there was not one single free space. "Have a seat, my friend and tell me your woes."

Eddie sat upon the larger cushion as the man faced him.

"I've never seen this many books, I mean except in the library."

"They're my friends, Eddie, these books; they speak to me and bring me the answers to my many questions about this life that we live. I have studied all my life about the purpose of existence and why we're all here. And still, I feel, despite the many, many years of study, I know only a little. And what I manage to learn, I use it to help others."

Eddie noticed a framed photograph on the table as well

as several others throughout the room of Jack posing with various men and women.

"Those are some of the folks whom I've met over the years. Some are teachers, others scholars, some religious leaders and political leaders. Some from the other side of the world and some who live just down the block. All in search of the same answers that I seek."

The man turned to face Eddie once again.

"But now you must tell me how I can help you."

Eddie was moved by the man's sincerity. It comforted him.

"It's my dreams. I think I'm losing sight of what is real and what's not."

Jack looked deeply into Eddie's eyes, almost as if he was reading his soul.

"Well, that is a very dangerous thing to do, Eddie. You must never confuse what is in front of you with what is not."

Eddie began to wonder if he sounded like some wacko to the old man; like someone who needed to be tied up in a straitjacket in Bellevue's psych ward.

"It's just, Jack…it's just that…I'm lonely…and sad…so I sleep…and when I sleep I dream."

Jack rose from his tiny stool and lit a candle.

"This is just for energy, Eddie. We must always be conscious of the light. Go on, go on."

Eddie felt like weeping as he continued.

"It's just that there's this woman, her name is Dalliancia. I'm in love with her and she loves me but she can't be with me. So, I dream. I dream of her and me, together, living happily and more and more each day, I've noticed how I prefer to sleep. I get to work late, sometimes, on some days I don't go to work at all. I just sleep and dream of her and I'm so happy, so happy that I don't want to wake up, do you understand? I just don't want to wake up. But then somehow my body or maybe my brain wakes me up and I just wait, just go through the day, waiting for the chance to sleep again, to dream again, about D. Dream about us. Because it's the only time…the only way that we can be together, understand?"

Jack returned to his seat listening carefully to each word, never betraying any shock or discomfort.

He just listened.

"Go on."

"So, my friend, Jennie, you know she's my good buddy, she knows about the dreams, I mean I told her, and she's my friend, and she covers for me at work when I oversleep. I mean, she watches my back and all, but she knows that it's not good for me, all this dreaming, and all that sleeping. She knows that D's not good for me. But Jennie's my friend. She wants the best for me. To be happy. So, that's why I'm here."

Jack sighed loudly as he stood and stared into the candle's jumpy flame.

"I've handled this type of problem before Eddie, so you're in luck. I can help you! All is not lost!"

The man laughed revealing again his empty smirk.

"Ha! I have met many who have come here, before you ,Eddie, who would prefer to sleep their lives away, rather than face their problems. And to tell you the truth Eddie, I don't blame them. Folks here in this area, in our community, Eddie, we face so many struggles and some, well they give up…but for those who do not give up, there is always hope…there is always the light."

Jack returned to his small bench.

"I'm going to show you a way to enter your dreams Eddie so that you can take control of them, before they control you!"

Eddie nearly rose as the man spoke.

"I don't get it…"

"Don't worry, Eddie. Stay calm. I'll explain. How long has it been since you've allowed yourself to waste your life on your delusions?"

Eddie met Dalliancia nearly a year ago and the dreams began almost two months after their first kiss.

"I don't know…maybe nine, ten months…"

Jack sprang from his chair creating a draft that nearly blew out the candle.

"What?! That's much too long, Eddie! Why, in only three months' time you can completely change the brain's entire circuitry. We must work now to fix this! Hurry!"

"I don't understand…what's going on?"

"Our brains are created to control our thoughts, our actions, and our movements but for the last 10 months, 10 months, Eddie, you have been teaching, commanding yourself to fall deeper and deeper into an abyss that one day you might not be able to get out of."

"I still don't get it."

"It's called defenseless dreaming, Eddie. Subconsciously you have been sending a signal to your brain to keep you in the dream state. Once you begin a habit such as this, it might be difficult to undo. Your brain has a power of its own. In its normal state it works in tandem and in balance with the rest of your body's functions to make sure that everything works properly. But you have subconsciously given it full reign to control you, to keep you where you think you are happiest but in fact you are close to death!"

Eddie felt an electric jolt shoot straight up his spine that almost made him cry out in horror.

"The brain is the strongest and most powerful muscle in your body and you have given it, for the last 9 or 10 months, even more power that you can ever imagine! Tell me more about your dreams, Eddie. Do you have nightmares as well?"

Eddie tried to recall his last dream but all he could see was Dalliancia standing near him, the lighted doorway, shining in her beautiful gown with her flowing dark hair that was wrapped like fertile grapevines around her arms and down to her thighs and legs and around her alluring charms.

"I don't remember. I just dream about what makes me happy. I dream of her."

"Think, Eddie. Try to remember if you saw anything that doesn't normally appear in your dreams with the girl…with Dalliancia."

Eddie closed his eyes and thought about last night and how the dream began, the same dream of D, as he would always see her, her translucent body, nearly twinkling, and she stood there in the entrance, his doorway, the entry to his heart, to their future, promising and shining, and he approached her, without his uniform on, but wearing his favorite white guayabera and white linen pants, barefoot, running towards her, she running towards him, embracing finally, and they would kiss, long and hard and tenderly and strip themselves of their clothing, their skin slightly touching, her body as soft and pliable as sugary caramelo, melting into each other, free from their obligations, finally free to be with each other.

But there was something as Eddie recalled the dread that lingered behind him as he kissed her, how its power pulled him away from D, her body feeling less substantial in his arms, almost as if she were fading, disappearing, as the darkness loomed closer, growing stronger, encircling them inside its suffocating desolation, trapping them in the dream.

"Yes, there was something, Jack, some kind of a power, like it was separating me from D."

Jack turned to pick up the candle.

"Eddie, that's it. That's your brain fighting to control you. If we don't do something soon, the next time that you fall asleep, you'll be lost forever in your subconscious mind with no hope for escape!"

Jack blew out the candle. "I'll be right back, Eddie. I have to fix some tea for us."

Eddie's heart raced. He remembered it clearly now, last night's dream and how it upset him and finally woke him. And how that fear propelled him towards the little shrine in his bedroom where he kept photographs of his parents killed by a drunk driver five years ago, on the West Side highway as they were returning home from a trip to the malls in New Jersey where they often go on the weekends to save on sales tax.

Their photos were kept neatly on top of the dresser, surrounded by some of their favorite things, including his father's red handkerchief and his mother's favorite hair brush, along with two cups of black coffee that he would make for them on occasion as he knew that somehow they were still there with him, watching over him, and keeping him safe.

Eddie was already dripping in sweat from the dream as he embraced the picture frames.

"Pa, Ma, you gotta help. Help me be strong and brave and help me to do the right thing."

Eddie gently kissed each framed photograph as he tried to shake off the weird energy of the dream and vowed to somehow win Dalliancia's reluctant heart once and for all.

"Here, Eddie, help me with this."

Jack entered with a tray that held a small burgundy ceramic teapot and its two matching cups.

"This is a special brew that will help you regain control and tame that wild brain of yours."

The tea's pungent aroma nearly took Eddie's breath away.

"Whew! What is this?"

Jack poured some tea for himself as he sat on the stool.

"Don't worry. It's not poison. It'll just make you relax. Relaxed enough so that you can experience lucid dreaming without really falling asleep."

Eddie sniffed at the cup again like a discriminating cat.

"You mean it's gonna make me dream, right now? I mean about D?"

"No, not quite."

Jack took a small sip from his share.

"I'll be right here all the time, Eddie, as well as with you as you dream, so that I can see, see through to what you are feeling, what you are thinking and dreaming, and to see what you're doing to command yourself to give up your free will. It's made from special herbs that can only be found in northern Africa. It's used by millions, over many centuries to experience the state of sleep, endless sleeplessness, without losing control. You remember that scene from Romeo and Juliet that you studied in high school? Where Juliet's nurse gets some herbs from the Friar to put Juliet into a deep sleep, but unfortunately Romeo thought that she was actually dead? It's the same as this."

Eddie placed the beverage down on the carpeted floor. He noticed that not only was this particular room so much more alive and revealing of its occupant than the living room, but its floor was carpeted with the kind of rug that Eddie only saw in fancy shops or department stores.

He retrieved his cup for fear of staining the remnant.

"Here's a coaster. Thank you for being careful. This is indeed my special magic carpet and once you take a sip of that tea, my friend, you'll understand what I mean."

Once again Eddie placed the drink beneath his nose and inhaled its vapors.

"I dunno Jack. I don't get it. You talk like my brain is bad or something, like it's my enemy. How can that be? How can something that is a part of me do me any harm?"

Again Jack sipped the drink, allowing its properties to prepare him for the dream session with his new client.

"I know that this all sounds a little weird, Eddie, all this talk about how your body can lose its equilibrium, and how harmful things can happen if you allow them to happen, even when you don't even realize it. That is why it is always so important to stay in the light. To venture out away from this beautiful, delicate balance, is one of the most treacherous and irreparable things that we can do."

Feeling reassured, Eddie began to drink the brew.

Hesitantly. But he drank.

"Now, just relax, Eddie. Take this stone." He handed Eddie a tiny, pointed crystal cube. "It's called a Herkimer Diamond and it's used to travel lucidly in our dreams. Here."

Jack retrieved a bit of the tea from his cup and sprinkled a few drops on the stone.

"But it needs water. Water is used for transforming energy, it's a conductor between light and energy; between here and now and what's to come."

Eddie noticed tiny bubbles of light lining the small, clear stone.

"It's beautiful. It looks like a real diamond."

"It is, Eddie. It's one of the purest diamonds that you will ever see. Nothing like you can find at Tiffany's. Now, just place it between your eyes, that divine spot, and breathe, Eddie. Breathe. Thank you for trusting me, for trusting yourself, Eddie. Now use that light to control yourself and what you are about to experience."

Instantly Eddie felt as if he was being lifted off the ground, weightless, almost feeling the same whenever he and Jennie would take the afternoon off to smoke some good weed.

"There, there, in just a moment, you will sleep, Eddie but you will have control and I will be here with you. On this you can count on…"

The old man's words faded into the glowing background of his recurring dream of Dalliancia, and soon he found her again, there in the splendorous entryway and this time, stars surrounded her or maybe they were tiny hummingbirds, twinkling as they sang, flitting around her light.

Eddie reached towards her and held her in his heart.

"I love you, D. Please be with me."

But like the night before, he felt something different, something lurking above and around them; muted, dark gray shades of a malevolence that lingered and bled between them.

"Dalliancia, where are you going?"

He felt her body crumble at once in his arms, molecule by molecule, as if she were made of sand. The shadow grew larger around them, nearly encircling their bodies as the birds began to pop, one by one, bursting like tiny soap bubbles with the prickly darkening force.

"Dalliancia!"

Eddie looked at her as she stood, disintegrating rapidly, losing her arm in his grip, and next her other arm, standing there like the Venus de Milo, limbless, her face frozen in a mask of horror.

"Eddie! Please don't let go!"

Eddie labored against the dark force, to rescue her and keep her, but it was as if he was grasping at empty air, as Dalliancia's legs began to disappear as well, until all that he held was her torso and her head.

"Eddie! Save me!"

Eddie now noticed that he too no longer had any arms with which to hold his true love.

"No! No!"

In an instant, a flash of light struck between them, seeping through a crack, splintered in the dream, like a vapor or a mist, and he saw the stalwart, black man, who wore a gold crown, brandishing a large steel silver sword and a crossbow over his shoulders. Across his broad bare chest he wore a pendant with a stone, riding atop a white horse, who also wore the stone in his headdress. The man's long thick curls and dark hair fell loosely around his shoulders under his crown, as he swung at the foe, that enveloped the disappearing couple, with his potent blade.

"Away! Away! I command you! Or I shall summon the Great Light! Away!"

Eddie now only held Dalliancia's head, still screaming for protection, as the warrior continued with the battle.

"Away! Away! This is not your place! Away!"

Eddie heard a shrieking noise, not a human scream, but more like that of an animal that was about to be butchered like the roosters and the pigeons that he once saw at the Vivero on West 126th Street and Amsterdam Avenue.

"Away! Away!"

The fighter continued until the dark diminished around the couple.

But it was too late.

Now Eddie held only Dalliancia's eyes in his hands and it horrified him.

"Ai! No! No!"

Eddie opened his eyes, finding himself lying on Jack's expensive rug.

It was eerily quiet as he rose up to his waist, noticing the relit candle on the table near him.

"Hi, I knew that you'd be awake by now. I fixed something for us to eat."

Eddie placed his hand on his heart, still racing from the dream, the nightmare or whatever the hell it was, as he got up on his feet, nearly stumbling back to the floor.

"Take it easy, Eddie," advised Jack as he re-entered with

a tray full of food. "You're still not equipped to recover from the experience. Please sit. Relax. Have something to eat. It will help you."

The tray was filled with bowls of steaming white rice, black beans and flavorful roasted chicken.

Eddie found himself ravished, for some odd reason not knowing where the hunger came from since he only arrived at the old man's place just a few minutes ago.

"It's getting late. You have to tell me what you saw."

Eddie looked out the window and saw that it was already night.

"How long have I been here? It was light out when I came."

Eddie abandoned his usual manners as he lustily attacked the food.

"Easy, there, kid. I don't want you to get indigestion."

Eddie looked up from the mangled chicken's thigh.

"I'm sorry. Why am I so hungry?"

"You were asleep, Eddie. For nearly three hours."

"What?"

"The dream world is different from the awake world, Eddie. Time is different, images are different, what we think is real, is not real at all. And what we think is not real, is really real."

Eddie began to remember what happened. The tea that he drank and how it made him feel.

And the dream, his dream of D and how she disappeared, and so did he, piece-by-piece, body part by body part, as the darkness enclosed them.

And then the hero arrived. To help them. To rescue them.

"Yes, now I remember."

Eddie recounted everything to Jack as they ate.

"You know Eddie, there are two different schools of thought in dream analysis. There's Freud, who interprets people and objects in our dreams as symbolic of the individual's state of mind and then there's Jung who categorizes by archetypes and the commonality of experience."

Eddie was nearly done with his meal as Jack served him another helping.

"Well, then, which was mine?"

"Well, Freud would have of course made the sexual connection between the warrior and his sword and horse and your sexual prowess. Whereas Jung would say that this particular archetype reflects the common, universal theme of good overcoming evil. I would say it's a little bit of both."

"But that guy. In the dream. Who was he? He looked like something outta of a Hercules movie. He didn't look like me at all, with his huge muscles and long black hair."

Eddie stared at Jack and remembered what he told him about having to stay strong in order to be able to rescue people.

"And you said that you'd be with me in the dream. I didn't see you!"

Jack finished his meal and returned the plate onto the tray.

"I was with you Eddie, or what you thought was me. What did you think of my horse?"

Eddie stopped eating as he pondered the impossibility of such a thing. But he remembered the African guerreros that his mother spoke of, and the ones that he saw in Jack's room--the brave trickster Esu, the great Ogun and Ochosi, the intrepid archer, and their ability to transcend time and space, and wondered if they were the ones who empowered Jack and saved his life.

"I told you Eddie, when we drank the tea together, that I would always be with you. I saw the imbalance taking control. Had I not arrived in time, your brain would have taken over completely and you would not have ever awoken. Do you understand? Do you see now that you have given it too much power? That now things, inside of your own body and mind are out of whack?"

With that Jack playfully slapped the back of Eddie's head.

"¡Despierta, hijo!"

Eddie stood up with difficulty, still groggy from the tea and sleep and now weighed down by the food.

"I don't know. I just wanna go home. It's late. I've been here too long already. I just wanna go home and sleep!" Eddie moved towards the door to leave.

"You mustn't fall asleep Eddie, not without some protection. You are still in a perilous and vulnerable state. You cannot trust your brain to stay in balance. Not yet."

"Then what should I do? Stay awake? That's insane! I need to sleep, everybody needs to sleep. What do you want me to do, take speed or something? This is all so idiotic! I should have never come here!"

Jack grabbed Eddie's forearm.

"Wait, Eddie, please. I'm not asking you to stay awake. I'm here to help you to stay in balance, to stay in check between the light and the dark. Don't you see that in your desire for Dalliancia you have allowed yourself to live in your dreams, to breathe, make love, and find happiness in your dreams? For lack of this one thing that you so long for, you have given up your right to live here in the light with the rest of us."

"That's fucked up! I gotta go…"

"Eddie, please. We're all in the same boat. We all must live our lives as best as we can, despite the torment and the pain of lost love. But we cannot allow that anguish to swallow us and make us not want to live!"

Eddie remembered his parents and the pain of solitude that he felt since their demise compounded now by his love for the unavailable woman.

"You don't understand. I'm happy when I dream. I don't feel any pain. I have Dalliancia and we're together, at last, without anyone or anything to bother us. She already left me. Why take my dreams away from me?"

"Eddie, I'm not taking anything away, I'm only trying to help you return to a normal state, even if it is an agonizing one. But I promise you the hurt does subside in time. It may never go away but like everything else it will be in balance. Joy, and pain…to have too much of one and not enough of the other, is not a whole existence."

Eddie wondered if his despair over his parents would ever subside.

"I don't know…I don't know."

Jack retrieved a Herkimer diamond pendant from the table.

"Wear this when you sleep tonight and from now on until we can resolve everything. It will protect you while you sleep but only if you call upon it when you need its help."

Jack placed the necklace over Eddie's head as he laid the stone upon the middle of his chest.

"It will provide you with the energy that you will need to overcome any oppression. But don't forget about the water. It will be the only way to travel in and out of your subconscious realms."

Eddie touched the stone firmly between his fingers already feeling its innate warmth, finding some strange comfort within.

"Please come again Eddie. I will help you to be happy in this world."

Jack walked Eddie to the door as they shook hands.

"Please send my regards to your friend Jennie. She is a good friend to you, Eddie."

Eddie nodded as he began to withdraw from the apartment.

"This is messed up! Maybe this is all a dream too!"

Before entering the elevator Eddie barely made out Jack's voice behind the closed door.

"Away! Away! Dark forces! Or I shall summon you to the Great Light!"

Eddie raced into the elevator knowing that everything that he had just experienced was not a dream at all and it terrified him.

Eddie wanted most to call Jennie when he got home that night but he was tired and sad.

Mostly sad.

After he was done showering, Eddie stood naked and stared down at Jack's pendant.

All he wanted was her and if the only way he could have her was in his dreams what harm would that do anybody?

Yeah, sure he was neglecting his job and everything else

but so what? He wanted out anyway, the constant grind and monotony was getting to him. He could use a little break; just him and D, just like in his dream where they would go and see her folks in DR and maybe even stay there and build their own little paradise.

Eddie picked up the brilliant stone and did his best to remember what Jack told him about its powers.

"That guy's nuts. All that shit about my brain taking over, that's bullshit! I'm the only one in control here…"

Eddie stared into the Herkimer diamond determined to reach Dalliancia that night as he went into the bathroom and sprinkled some water over it.

"Please take me to her again. I need her."

Eddie placed the pendant around his neck and slid under the bed sheets. In that moment he realized that his real life was actually his nightmare! Having to sneak around with D, meeting her in flea-bag hotel rooms, seeing her with her husband and their kids in the store, laughing and hugging, and loving on one another, and now, now, she left him! That was a nightmare!

But this, this deep sleep, was lovely, was exhilarating, it was living! It was life! It was love!

As he surrendered to the sleep Eddie tried to remember what is was that Jack told him about the lucid dreaming, about how you can control your actions or your thoughts while you're dreaming or something like that, like when you realize that indeed you are dreaming and how in your dream state you can use this awareness to change things.

The sleep continued to overpower him as he began to trail off into D's arms and there she was, appearing before him as always in her sheer white gown, curly ringlets of stars surrounding her like a halo, an angel, his angel, as he walked towards her embrace.

"D, I'll never let you go, never!"

Eddie remembered what Jack told him about being aware inside the dream as he removed the pendant and placed it on the pliant ground beneath their feet.

"I want to be with you forever, D," he promised her. "I want to stay here with you forever."

As they kissed, Eddie could feel the energy surging between them as if they were truly, truly alive! For the first time, he felt that he was now able to let go of the fear, the fear of losing her and never achieving his dreams and he was now determined, more than ever, to live here inside the dream with her for an eternity.

"Come on, D, let's go."

Dalliancia never said a word to him as they walked hand in hand. Or were they walking?

They were actually floating, gliding further and further inside the dream, down a cobble-stoned path that was lit in shades of translucent blues and coral. Eddie now knew he was in control of himself and what he truly wanted, as he felt her heartbeat in his hand, and now he was completely aware of his surroundings as never before and he felt strong and became bolder with each step, happily forgetting his other world, his other life that made him so, so unhappy.

"Come, D. Let's go find our little house."

And as if he willed it, a small tropical island appeared before them; the deep turquoise Caribbean sea surrounding their bodies, and a tiny white bungalow in the distance, made of flowers with Ceibas and flamboyan trees encircling the home, and as they moved closer to the delicate structure he could feel Dalliancia being pulled away.

"Don't worry, D. It's okay. This is what I've been dreaming of. This is our home."

Eddie gently moved her closer as they entered its brightly lit abode. Inside the flowers bloomed rapturously creating a sanctum of beauty and radiance.

"Look, D. It's heaven."

The couple stood hand in hand as Eddie could sense her trepidation.

"There's nothing to be afraid of, D. I'm in control now and we'll never go back."

Dalliancia stared at him with her eyes tearing, growing larger with terror.

"Please, D, there's nothing to worry about."

In that moment the flowers began to wither before them, each one dying as if they were poisoned, as the dark phantom covered their light—its potency growing with each dying bloom.

"What's this?"

Eddie turned to Dalliancia who was also now disappearing.

"D! No!"

Soon all that was left of Dalliancia were her eyes, weeping; her tears, droplets, suspended in mid-air like dangling transparent earrings.

"No! D! Oh, God, no!"

Eddie thought hard to remember what Jack told him, but as hard as he tried to gain control, the harder it was to remember what to do, slipping at every step as if he were walking on an ice skating rink like the one in Central Park.

Eddie looked down at his feet as he noticed that indeed what was once firm ground had dissolved, and he now stood upon what looked like a floor made of large eyes—Dalliancia's eyes!

"No!"

Eddie hurried to steady himself, as he tried to find his way out of the dream, back into his real world, but with each step he grew weaker and more defenseless against the dark force that now overpowered him

"What is this? Please help me!"

Eddie was able to make out two approaching figures.

"Please, go away!"

One of the figures reached out to him, touching his arm as if to summon him to rise.

"Please! No!"

Eddie looked up and to his amazement and relief saw that they were his parents, whom he had not dreamed about since he met D.

"Pa! Ma! Please help me."

They remained silent as they helped him to his feet.

"I wanna go back now. I wanna wake up."

His parents walked with Eddie, placing him between them.

"Where are we going? Are you taking me home?"

Eddie looked at the two figures on either side of him and saw that they were no longer his parents but monsters, grotesque and scaly.

"Get away from me. Get away!"

Despite their combined stronghold Eddie was able to

escape from the beasts as he ran upon a ground that now seemed different.

Eddie looked down at his feet and noticed that they were now bleeding from the spiky tiny thorns that now covered his dream path.

"No! Please! Help!"

Eddie observed that the air had become stale making it difficult to take a breath.

He reached out his arms and touched what seemed like a wall and another wall until he was completely encased inside a glass box.

"Help! Help! Get me out!"

Eddie looked through his transparent prison and saw his sleeping self safe in his bedroom on his bed just as he had left himself before deciding to give up his real world in exchange for his dream world with Dalliancia.

"Wake up! Wake up! Wake up!"

Eddie continued to pound against the walls as he screamed at his sleeping self to arise.

His feet continued to bleed, as did his fists as he wrestled to return to his former life. From inside his dream, Eddie saw Jennie as she entered the bedroom holding the extra set of keys that Eddie made for her on those days when he would need her to wake him.

"Thank God! Jennie! Can you hear me? Wake me up! I'm stuck inside the dream! Jennie! Jen!"

Jennie moved to his bed and began to tug on his arm.

"Man, I don't care if I'm dreaming about Halle Berry. If I heard someone trying to come into my apartment, you know my ass'd be up! Yo, Ed, it's me Jen. Wake up, bro. It's almost twelve and we got a lot of packages to deliver."

Jennie moved to the living room and saw that Eddie had left his UPS uniform sprawled on the couch.

"Eddie, my man, you are a slob!"

Jennie carefully picked up the uniform and folded it neatly as she surveyed the rest of the apartment.

"Yo, Ed, my man! I don't wanna be coming into your crib like this, but you have got to wake your butt up!"

Jennie found the flyer that she gave Eddie about the spiritual guy.

"Looks like my man finally took some of my advice."

Jennie placed the ad on the sofa as she reentered the bedroom.

"Yo, man, I hate to do this but you give me no choice."

Jennie pulled at his arms, nearly tossing his entire body off the bed.

"Yo, Ed, come on now! It's time to wake up, sleeping beauty! Come on, man, I ain't playing! I can't keep covering for you like this! We're both gonna get into trouble!"

Jennie shook him again with even greater force.

"Yo, man! I know that you like those dreams of yours but you gotta wake up! Start living your life!"

Jennie angrily pulled the blanket off his body.

"Eddie! Eddie!"

Eddie's bleeding feet from the dream were now bleeding in the real world soaking the mattress with red stickiness.

"Shit man, what the fuck happened??"

"Eddie! Please! Wake up! What's wrong with you man! Wake up!"

But Eddie could not wake up as much as Jennie tried.

He saw her from inside the glass prison. "I'm stuck inside the dream, Jen! Help me!"

Jennie ran into the bathroom and returned with a towel as she tended to Eddie's ravaged feet.

"Yo, man what's the fuck is this? What's wrong with you? Eddie, please wake up!"

Eddie, trapped inside the cube, was powerless. "Jennie! Jennie! Can't you hear me! Please help me!"

But as loud as he yelled he knew that Jennie could not hear him, that she would never hear him.

After some time, Jennie managed to control the bleeding as she raced back into the living room.

"What the fuck am I gonna do?"

Jennie pulled out her cell phone.

"I can't call the cops, not with all this shit. They'll fucking blame it on me! Shit! Shit!"

Jennie circled the room and then re-entered Eddie's bedroom.

"Eddie, what did you do? Wake up! Where the fuck are you? Can't you hear me?"

Jennie bent low towards the body checking for a pulse.

"You're alive, but how do I reach you, man? Eddie! Eddie! Where are you?"

Jennie remembered the spiritual guy and wondered if he had anything to do this with Eddie's condition. She ran back and found the ad and lost no time to dial the number.

"Yeah, man. This is Eddie's friend, Jennie. What the fuck did you do to him?"

After a minute of explanation Jennie learned what had transpired between Jack and Eddie.

"Well, I think you better get your butt over here real quick because I can't wake him and he's fucking bleeding from his feet!"

Jack reassured Jennie of his sincerity.

"Your friend can hear you, Jennie. Just keep talking to him until I get there. He lost his will and now he has allowed his brain to live his life inside his dreams, do you understand?"

"Nah, man, I don't get it but please come. I'll keep talking to him."

"Jennie, listen to me. Do you see a pendant around his neck?"

"What?"

"A pendant. It's a stone, a special type of diamond that I gave to Eddie to protect himself."

"Nah, man, I don't see nothing."

"Talk to him, Jennie. Ask him where the stone is. Tell him to find the stone or get as close to it as possible. Do you understand?"

"What stone? I don't know. This is fucking unbelievable!"

"It's the only way that we can help him until I get there, Jennie. I know it sounds incredible but please just get him to find the stone!"

"Okay, okay the stone. I'll tell him."

Jennie sat on the bed as she moved closer to Eddie.

"Listen, buddy, this guy, Jack, he just told me that you can hear me and I'm praying to God that you can, Ed."

Jennie looked into Eddie's face and noticed that it had grown considerably paler since she first walked in.

"Hang in there, Ed, Jack is coming. He said he can help you out. But you gotta help him too, you understand? You gotta want to come back, even if it means losing D. But I promise you, buddy, I promise you're gonna find somebody else. Somebody just as sweet and just as nice and just as beautiful. I promise you. And you're gonna find her and she'll be there waiting for you, because that's how it works, Ed, we're all just waiting for each other, you understand? Can you hear me, Eddie?"

Eddie heard her and he knew she was right. She was right all along.

It was time to come back home.

Jennie looked down and noticed that Eddie's eyes began to move slightly.

"Yes, yea, that's right, Ed. Now, I don't know where you are right now, buddy, but wherever you are I want you to find that stone, the stone that Jack gave you. I want you to go to it and put it back around your neck, you understand? Everything's gonna be just fine, Eddie, just fine."

Jennie pulled the blanket closer to her friend's body, fitting it tightly around his body, holding him like an infant.

"Stay strong, okay? I know it's hard, this world, this life, without your folks, without D, but there's a lot of love out there, Ed, and one day you'll find it. I promise. But right now I just need you to find that stone, you hear me?"

Eddie heard every word as Jennie spoke, trying to remember where he had left the stone.

Eddie still felt it inside him, the will to live, barely there, but he felt it now and he would use it to get out and search for his true life's destiny.

Soon the clear walls began to fade around him as he remembered what Jack told him about lucid dreaming and taking control of his actions.

"I will find that stone. I will."

Eddie tried to retrace his steps.

But, with each step, he felt the emptiness still weighing heavily upon him. He tried to reason with himself. With his brain.

"Please, I made a mistake. I want to go back."

Eddie continued as he finally spotted the pendant on the road where he and Dalliancia had walked upon.

"It's all just a dream. I get it now. Just a stupid dream. I want to live again."

He saw the stone, just a few feet away, lying there, feeling its energy even from where he stood and he raced towards it. But he felt the resistance and remembered his brain and the power that he had given it.

"It's time to let go and bring things back to where they were."

But the force was relentless as Eddie felt it nearly punch the wind out of him just as he was about to bend to pick up the pendant.

"Don't you get it? I want to get out! I want to wake up!

Life is a good thing! It's a good thing! Now wake the fuck up!"

But Jack was right.

Once these things were out of balance it was difficult to make them right again.

Eddie looked down at his hands now covered in boils making it difficult to grip the diamond.

"Jennie! Can you hear me? Please help!"

The blisters grew more prominent throughout his body

as Eddie began to feel weak.

"Jennie! Help!"

Jennie noticed Eddie's body trembling. His arms were covered in what looked like mosquito bites.

"He can't get out! He's stuck!"

The intercom rang from downstairs as Jack announced his fortuitous arrival.

"Come quick, man. We're losing him!"

Jennie returned to Eddie's body as she placed wet towels on his arms.

"Help is on the way, Ed. Hang in there!"

Eddie continued to reach for the stone, which teasingly moved away from him, and he remembered his parents and how they would often tell him how he should never give up on his dreams. No matter what, even when things were at their worst, he must persist and be happy.

Eddie realized just how unhappy his life had become in wanting something that was beyond his grasp as he felt his body inching closer and closer to the stone.

How his dreams of Dalliancia were not rooted in any reality that was attainable and how he knew that he had to give up on her and allow her to be happy despite his deep love for her.

Eddie was within reach of the stone, feeling its pulse warming his fingertips. He knew that his parents would have been so disappointed for their son, their only son, to waste his time on idle fantasies and how they would have encouraged him to instead seek happiness elsewhere because somewhere it was waiting for him, just for him, just as Jennie said. In that moment Eddie knew in his heart that this was true, as true as gold, as he held the stone in his hands and felt a wave of safety come over him.

Jennie opened the door as Jack arrived and he stood there for a moment out of breath.

"Come on, there's no time to waste."

Jennie led him to Eddie's sleeping body as Jack checked his pulse.

"He's warm. He has the stone."

Jack sat on a chair near the bed and removed an identical amulet that laid beneath his sweater.

"I'm going in."

"What do you mean? Going in? Where are you going? Am I gonna have to get another guy to save you too? Nah, man, you stay right here with me and you help me get this poor boy outta there."

Jack had already returned from the bathroom where he placed the now wet diamond stone on his temple.

"You don't understand, young lady. There's no other way to save him. Trust me."

Jack instantly fell into a deep sleep meditating on Eddie, searching for Eddie, entering Eddie's subconscious through the crystal. Jennie continued to hold Eddie's hand, feeling his vitality return.

"Hang in there, Ed. Before you know it we'll be hanging out again smoking boo. And you know I didn't tell you. Me and Caridad, we're moving in together. Yep! She's great, Ed. I know we're gonna be happy. And it's gonna happen to you too, man. You'll see. So you just hang in there."

Jennie knew that it was best to wait until Eddie returned from his coma before she told him about Dalliancia, who called her late last night from the Dominican Republic.

"Please tell him, Jen, for me, that I love him. But I love my family."

Jennie knew that Eddie would be devastated by the news.

"I meant to tell him before in the diner. We left right after I saw him. Orlando and I had planned it for months. We left the store with our cousin, Pepe. It's better that we're here, at home, with my parents. The city is too depressing for me, for us. Please let Eddie know that I'm sorry."

Jennie wondered how in hell she was gonna break the news to Eddie. First D breaks up with him and now she leaves the fucking country!

Jennie looked down at Eddie's body nearly restored to its former life.

"I promise you Eddie. Everything's gonna be alright. And that's a good thing ain't it?"

Eddie held on tightly to the stone as he noticed that the light was beginning to fade.

"Please, please, Ma, Pa, please get me back home."

In that moment, Eddie felt a familiar sensation. The same energy that produced electricity in his body when he first met Jack.

"Get back! Get back or I will summon the Great Light!"

It was the Great Warrior King riding triumphantly on his white steed. Eddie looked above and saw them along the periphery of a dream that enslaved him.

"The balance must be restored. Return to your space now!"

With that the great soldier angled his crossbow at the dark force as it began to fight back, encircling the man and his horse with its dominance.

"Eddie! Move away. Get into the light."

Using the power that the stone provided, Eddie ran to an area that was indeed flooded with light, which increased in intensity with each arrow from the rescuer's weapon. Finding no water near him, Eddie spat on the stone and waited for the transformation.

"Stay there, Eddie! Soon you'll be home!"

The power dueled with the pair as Eddie began to feel awake again, alive once again as the stone grew hotter and hotter in his hands, nearly scorching his palm.

"I can feel it now! I can feel it!"

Eddie looked at the celestial soldier and his stallion, as they seemed to falter against the weight of the dominant energy.

"I'll help you!"

"Stand back, Eddie. It'll swallow you again. You're too weak to fight! Stay back and soon you'll be home!"

The warrior released yet another arrow at the impending doom, as it seemed to retreat momentarily.

Eddie knew that he had to do something to save them, to save all of them, as the light grew exponentially in size around him.

"Stand right there, Eddie and soon you'll be home."

Eddie felt himself lifted by the light as he soon found and stood upon the road that brought him there when he first fell asleep, moving further and further away from the conflict within.

Eddie saw himself up high in the dream, floating, flying, above the great battle when he hurled the stone, hot and nearly breathing, a life of its own, towards his hero.

"Jack! Here! Catch! This will help you!"

Instantly Eddie woke up and saw Jennie standing over him.

"Eddie! Eddie!"

She held him and pulled him upright to a seated position in the bed.

"You're back, Ed!"

Eddie looked around the room as he trembled and vibrated from the dream, his fingertips and his soul, numb and raw from holding the stone and returning to life.

"Jennie! What happened? I fell asleep. I wanted to sleep forever, Jen. I wanted to be with D forever. I'm sorry. I'm sorry."

Eddie wept openly into Jennie's arms as she held him and he held her, and onto this life and this reality once and for all.

"I know I can't be with her, Jen. I know. I promise I won't do it again."

Jennie rocked Eddie in his arms, steadying, firmly anchoring him to his life.

"Go ahead and cry, Ed. That's what you're supposed to do. You just take your time."

Jack's body remained still in the chair as Eddie remembered the stone and the warrior.

"It's him, Jen. Jack entered my dream to rescue me. Jen, we gotta get him out. He's fighting my brain for me."

"Fighting your brain? But you're here now. You ain't asleep. How? I don't get it."

"I don't get it either but he's still in there!" Eddie bent to whisper into Jack's ear.

"Come on, Jack. It's time to get out. You did your job. The nightmare is over! I'm here. I made it. You won! We won!"

Jennie walked over to the men. "Honey, if you're trying to wake somebody up, you gotta speak up!" Jennie stood before the seated man and took a deep breath. "Jack! Wake the fuck up! Wake the fuck up now!"

Jennie turned to a mystified Eddie.

"Come on, man, you wanna save him? Then you're gonna have to scream with me!"

Eddie knew that Jennie was right as he yelled as loudly as he could.

"It's over, Jack! Come on, wake up! Wake the fuck up!"

The two continued yelling as Jack began to move his closed eyes back and forth beneath the closed lids.

"Look, something's happening."

Again the pair continued until they noticed Jack struggling to open his eyes.

"Come on, man, you can do it. You can do it!"

As they held him, Jennie noticed a pool of blood soaking his sweater.

"Yo, Eddie, Look!"

"Get some towels from the bathroom, Jen. He's hurt."

Jack opened his eyes as Eddie held him.

'That's right, Jack. You can do it. Come on."

Jennie returned with the towels as she removed Jack's sweater and pressed hard on his chest to stop the bleeding.

"Come on, Jack, you're almost there. You're almost home."

Jack opened his eyes, revealing a fatigue that comes after fighting a great battle.

"Eddie, Eddie," whispered Jack. "Are you okay?"

Jack collapsed into Jennie's arms.

"He's gonna be okay now, Jack. Eddie got out!"

Eddie lifted the old man from her arms and placed him on the bed.

"Thanks Jack. I owe you."

Jack raised his arm slightly.

"We'll talk about my fee later."

***

In the days and weeks that followed, Jennie and Eddie took turns nursing Jack back to health and learning more about his transformative powers and his ability to travel between reality and the dream state.

"I guess I was born with it, and I try to help people like Eddie who lose their desire to live their lives."

Jennie fed him the sopa de pollo that Caridad prepared especially for the old man.

"But I don't get it, Jack. I just don't get it."

Jack, his strength nearly restored, savored the soup's spices as he explained.

"My dear, Jennie, sometimes I don't understand it either but all I know is that with a little bit of help from the crystal and a little bit of help from the Light anything is possible."

Jack winked at Jennie as Eddie returned from his afternoon delivery shift to take care of Jack.

Eddie had already learned about D's departure and secretly he was relieved. Although his heart was broken he knew that one day it would heal.

And in time, Eddie was able to sleep normally again and began to dream about his parents again, who spoke to him and told him how much they loved him. Jennie and Eddie even talked about starting up their own delivery service. They would start small, with a little truck of their own, using the list of customers that they nurtured over the years. With the money that Eddie saved and a small business loan that Jennie applied for at the credit union, they knew that this was one dream that might come true.

"Hey, look at what I got here!"

Eddie removed a small box from inside the Kmart plastic shopping bag.

"It's an alarm clock!"

Eddie activated its siren, nearly deafening them.

"Man, if that don't wake your ass up, Ed, I don't know what will!"

Eddie laughed as did Jennie while Jack continued with Caridad's savory broth.

And they all agreed that life, real life, was indeed worth waking up for.

Author's Note

As a native New Yorker, I've met a lot of interesting people in my time and have had some remarkable experiences.

All of the stories in my book, *Urban Folk Tales*, are based upon many of these encounters, some of which were so extraordinarily unbelievable that I had to use the fictitious components of magical and spiritual realism to understand and explain them.

"The Erasable Man," was inspired by a handsome, young, and dark-skinned man who I met through a colleague from work, who invited me to join them at a nearby club for drinks and dancing. As we danced, he removed his jacket and rolled up his sleeves to cool himself off from the crowded dance floor. I noticed a long, white scar etched on his left forearm. "Are you ok?" He smiled unashamedly and proudly pointed to the pale stripe that contrasted starkly against his bare, brown arm. "Oh, this? I'm fine," he proclaimed. "I'm just erasing myself with a number two pencil." Was he crazy, I wondered, as I made my way home that night or just simply, brutally practical and honest.

As someone who experienced racism, I understood why he would want to erase himself, (yes, even in New York City racism is still prevalent. Recently, I was asked, "where are you from?" with the implication being that I don't look like, or sound like from someone who is from "here." Or the time-often attack that I "don't sound, look or act Puerto Rican").

I completely understood how easier my life, my family's lives, and my friends' lives would be if we were white. How all of the wonderful opportunities, from getting a good paying job, to hailing a cab, or to simply walk the streets at night without being harassed by the cops, could be ours if we could, like the young man at the night club, change our skin color (my father, a dark-olive skin man, or "trigueño," would tell me about the many times that he got hit in the head by an Irish cop's billy club for speaking Spanish in public or for just existing when he arrived to New York City in the late 40s; "Chico! This is America!" bellowed the police officer as he aimed for my father's skull…yes, indeed, it was and still is).

That memory from the nightclub was so incredibly vivid that I was sure that one day it would become a story. In "The Erasable Man," I tell the story about Bobby Jose Iglesias, a Black, Cuban American college student, who yearns for acceptance in a city, that, like many other cities in the world, just can't get past the surface. While at work, at a Duane Reade pharmacy in downtown Manhattan, Bobby discovers a box of "magic pencils" that holds the promise of finally living a free life. He quickly grabs this opportunity and begins to erase his former life and replace it with one that supposedly would bring him the inner joy and peace that he longed for.

In "The Erasable Man," I also wanted to address the issue of racism in the Hispanic culture, where lighter skin Hispanics get the better things in life than their darker skin counterparts; an unspoken truth in a culture that prides itself on being unbiased and not at all racist.

In time, Bobby soon realizes that undergoing such a radical transformation holds its own disturbing consequences which ultimately lead him to a place where the color of his skin holds no importance at all.

One day, after I had just finished visiting my mother in Washington Heights, I made my way back home to Inwood, and stopped at a nail salon on West 204th and Broadway where I decided to treat myself to a manicure. The salon was one that I frequented from time to time, and it was during these visits, that I got to know its owner and employees. The proprietor was a woman who came to this country from South Korea in the early 1980s, and most of her employees were from various parts of Asia and Latin America. The owner immediately sat me down in front of a young Hispanic girl who gently grabbed both my hands and dipped them leisurely into the tiny bowls of warm water before me to soften the nails so that she could begin her work. After she was done, she asked me to select a shade from the expansive palette of nail polish colors; as always, I opted for the clear. As she stroked each nail with the tiny brush, I noticed that she was making the sign of the cross. "¿Estás haciendo la señal de la cruz en mis uñas?" ("Are you making the sign of the cross on my nails?"). She did not look up to answer me, choosing instead to smile sweetly as she continued with the ritual.

That powerful gesture became "The Manicurist," a story about Inez Jaramillo, a young immigrant and clairvoyant from El Salvador, who lives in Washington Heights and works at a nail salon owned by Su-Jin Sung, a South Korean immigrant.

Inez's story is told both in the present day and with the use of flashbacks about her life in El Salvador where her family faced political and religious persecution at the hands of an American-backed oligarchy that sanctioned oppressive, socio-political institutions such as the Catholic Church as manifested in the story by the cruel Father Everett.

The story also speaks about Inez's innate gift of prophecy. Her visions come to her as she holds and works on the hands of her clients at the nail salon; making the sign of the cross on the nails of those for whom she foresees misfortune; and thus, protecting them from what's to come. It was because of this spiritual aptitude that her family decided to send Inez off to America to protect her and her talent from their tormentors who devised to manipulate Inez's psychic ability to capture the "freedom fighters," some of whom were Inez's relatives, who fought against the regime.

In addition, a historical reference is made in the story to the 1990 "Happy Land Social Club" fire. Inez uses her gift to advise her friend Lourdes against meeting her jealous boyfriend at the "Dream Land Social Club," a nightclub frequented by the Hispanic community in New York City. But Inez's words go unheeded as her prediction about Lourdes' demise at the club is tragically fulfilled (87 Latinos perished by a fire set by a jealous boyfriend at "Happy Land" making it one of the deadliest fires in New York City, second to the Triangle Shirtwaist Factory fire).

By the end of the story, Inez's love for her family, her country, and Su-Jin, forces her to take an irrevocable step that finally returns her home.

"Laura and the Kickboxer" is one of the truer and most buoyant stories in the collection. It's a love story about Laura Miranda, a young Puerto Rican college graduate who is wasting her life on a married man and an unfulfilling job, and who longs to become a professional singer, and David

"El Caballo" Calderon, a former Puerto Rican kickboxer champion who wasted his life on drugs and longs for a comeback, both professional and personally. What starts out as a mild infatuation turns into a life-changing and lifesaving saga that promises the hope of a new beginning, both for the lonely, young girl and the earnest ex-fighter.

Among the other characters in the story are Mickey "The Mouth" Maldonado, a big-time numbers runner in the Bronx, who employs David to "muscle" his customers to pay unpaid debts, and his sidekick Pete. Both Mickey and Pete are Runyonesque characters who add humor and pathos to the story.

Whether it's Bobby in the "The Erasable Man, or Inez in the "The Manicurist," Laura and David in "Laura and the Kickboxer," or any of the other characters in "Waiting for Dr. Wu," "Hav-a-Cup of Coffee," and "The Man Who Dreamed Too Much," each of these stories are both personal and fantastical in their origins and themes. I hope that I was able to make them worthy of being both memorable and indelible in the collective social consciousness.

Y. Rodriguez, August 2022

Acknowledgements

Sending my love to my siblings, Joseph, Evelyn, William, and Felicita, for their support and encouragement through the years. And I'd like to thank my cousin, Carmen Rodgers and my sister, Evelyn Marron, for helping me to proofread the manuscript and finding those pesky little typos that are often missed. I also wanted to acknowledge my mentor, Crystal Field, for giving me the room in which to grow as a playwright and as a writer, and to Mary Jane Di Massi for first introducing me to Crystal. Last, I'd like to acknowledge my publishers at Read Furiously Press, Samantha Atzeni and Adam Wilson, who believed in my worth as a prose writer with this publication—I will always remember their reassuring praise and confidence in my abilities.

Photo Credit: Olivia Rodriguez

Born in Manhattan to Puerto Rican parents. Y. Rodriguez is a published, produced, and award-winning playwright and director who has had her plays produced in Off-Broadway theater companies throughout Manhattan. Ms. Rodriguez is also a published poet, and a professional musician and songwriter who performs with her band, AYOKA, in venues throughout Manhattan and Brooklyn.

Scan here to find more about Y. Rodriguez

A Note to our Furious Readers

From all of us at Read Furiously, we hope you enjoyed our latest title, *Urban Folk Tales: Stoires.*

At Read Furiously, we wish to add an active voice to the world we all share by nurturing positive change in our local and global communities. It is with this in mind that we pledge to donate a portion of these book sales to causes that are special to Read Furiously. These causes are chosen with the intent to better the lives of others who are struggling to tell their own stories.

The causes we support encourage a sense of social responsibility associated with the act of reading. Each cause has been researched thoroughly, discussed openly, and voted upon carefully by Read Furiously editors.

To find out more about who, what, why, and where Read Furiously lends its support, please visit our website at readfuriously.com/charity

Happy reading and giving, Furious Readers!

**Read Often, Read Well,
Read Furiously!**

www.ingramcontent.com/pod-product-compliance
Lightning Source LLC
Chambersburg PA
CBHW070509300726
48975CB00007B/2387